My Ratchet Secret 5 – The Resurrection

Disclaimer:

The Fat Lady Ain't Sung

Where the hell am I?

I woke up in a state of confusion. It appeared that I was in a hospital bed, but how did I get here? There was a weird sensation on the left side of my head. And I couldn't understand why my vision was so distorted. I attempted to touch the area that felt weird. However, I could barely move my arm due to the extensive number of machines I was hooked up to. After a bit of maneuvering, I managed to pat my head. It felt like it was gone! Despite my entire skull, along with the left side of my face being bandaged up, I could still feel a distinct indentation. Panic immediately set in. For the life of me I couldn't remember how I'd gotten here. From what I could tell, it must have been something pretty serious. Did I have an accident? Did someone try to hurt me? I tried to scream but the tube in my throat wouldn't allow it. The drugs that had been administered had me so heavily sedated that I couldn't get up if wanted to. I don't know what happened or how I ended up here but make no mistake, Pebbles is alive bitches!

Getting On With Life

If anyone would have told me that I could one day be happy again I would have called you a damn liar. I had lost everything. The person whom I believed to be my loving wife was an imposter. I was beaten to near death. I'd lost my son, my sanity, my will to live. And yet despite it all, God saw that I still persevered. It's taken a lot to get to this point, and I take nothing for granted.

I have my son back and we are working on making up for lost time and building a relationship. I have a new lady in my life. And yes she's a real woman this time. I wasn't playing any games this time around. I had her checked out extensively. Especially considering she would eventually move in with me and AJ. I ran her through every

4

background check possible before I allowed her to lay her head in the same home my son resides in. He has been enough and I refuse to put him in harm's way. My gut told me Jennifer was on the up and up, and I was right. Some people question how I was able to move on so soon after the tragedy that AJ and I suffered. The answer is quite simple. Jennifer was my saving grace while I was in therapy. She is smart, understanding, loving, and most of all she could empathize with my situation. In many ways we saved each other. It didn't take long for me to develop feelings for her. And unlike when I was with Pebbles, I never feel like she's hiding anything. It's like we were soul mates destined to be together. The way our paths crossed I have no doubt in my mind that this is the person I was meant to be with.

There was a time when I wouldn't have rested, knowing that Pebbles was still alive. She'd been shot in the face by my son but somehow her wicked soul managed to survive. She was comatose in Mercy Hospital under police surveillance. When, and if she ever wakes up I pray that justice is served.

These days I'm just happy to be alive myself and want nothing more than to move on with my life. I figured if her crazy ass didn't die that means the universe has something far worse in store for her. Who was I to question it?

I was jarred from my thoughts by the phone ringing. I glanced at the caller ID to see that it was Dorian. He had played a huge part in us catching Pebbles and finding my son, but he still hadn't gotten over the fact that she was still alive.

"Hello"

"What's up?" Dorian replied.

"Shit, I guess you heard the news huh?"

"Yeah, that Pebbles is awake. Damn, I wish your son would have finished that damn shim off," he spat.

"They got her now. And she's not going anywhere," I assured him.

"I don't know how the hell you can be so calm. You must have forgotten who we are talking about. As long as Pebbles is alive she is a threat to society. I'm still having nightmares behind what she did to Fallyn. I can't get that image of her lying there out of my mind. Me and my wife have separated behind this bullshit. I just don't get you," Dorian replied in disgust.

He was actually starting to piss me off. This shit he was sitting over there whining about was a cake walk compared to the hell Pebbles had put me through.

"Have you forgotten that she left me for dead? All the years she was out there with my child, she killed my sister. Shall I go on?"

Sensing the agitation in my voice he tried to back pedal.

"Aye man, I didn't mean it like that. I know you done been through far worse...."

"Exactly," I cut him off midsentence. "I've been held captive too many years by this nightmare. To the point of me trying to commit suicide. I'm in a healthy place now and I refuse to give her any more energy."

"I feel you. I'm just not over that shit."

"Don't get me wrong, I'm far from being over it. I'm still going to counseling. But as of now my main focus is making up for lost time with my son. I have a good woman in my corner that's helping me get through this. We gon be alright."

"I can respect that. I'm glad to hear you are working through this. I need to take a page from your book, my ass is still running scared," he joked in an attempt to lighten up the mood.

I laughed, "I feel you man. But just know that they are watching her around the clock. She's woke but she's damn near on her death bed. I don't think we have to worry about Pebbles hurting anyone else."

"I hope you're right."

What's Really Going On?

"I'm just saying girl, I don't know how you do it," Keke announced shaking her head. "You better than me."

She and Jennifer had been friends since their sophomore year of college despite their personalities being polar opposites. Jennifer was the slightly nerdy, girl next door type. While Keke was as ratchet as they came.

Jennifer was a soft spoken thirty-four-year-old brainiac. Her ideal weekend consisted of curling up with a good novel, binge watching reruns of Jeopardy or catching up on the latest documentary on quantum physics. Her sandy brown high bun, freckled nose and horn rimmed glasses added to her almost school girl appearance. Yet she still had an understated sexiness about her despite the toll life had taken on her.

Keke resembled a young Chaka Khan. Numerous tatts decorated her buttery walnut complexion. She had a dazzling white smile, and her thick, lush, naturally curly mane was as wild and free as her spirit.

The unlikely pair would eventually bond because of their differences, not in spite of them.

In Jennifer Keke found balance and stability. Unlike many of her other basic ass friends, she had her shit together and helped to keep her grounded whenever her party girl ways tried to take over.

Keke was fiercely loyal and had helped Jennifer get though a rough period in her life.

Her lighthearted humor and laid back demeanor helped Jennifer to loosen up and have fun. She taught her how to not take life so serious, and to take time to smell the roses. They were a perfect balance for each other.

Jennifer shook her head and took a sip of her peach margarita as she listened to her friend's usual critique of Adrian.

"I don't know why you have to be so hard on him," she responded.

"Because I want you to be happy. You've been through enough shit for a lifetime," Keke replied with concern in her voice. "This was a big step y'all took. I just want you to make sure you know what you are getting into."

"I know it's a big step, but I keep telling you, I am happy. I love Adrian. He was so supportive of me during that bad time. I don't know how I would have made it many days without his encouragement."

Jennifer's eye's beamed just talking about Adrian. The bad time she was speaking of was the time she spent in group counseling. Her mother, father, and younger sister were all killed as the result of a carjacking gone horribly wrong. Aside from being grief stricken, she'd become severely depressed, resulting in a failed suicide attempt. When she met Adrian he was recovering from alcohol addiction and as well as the attempt he'd made on his own life.

"I guess…. You know I think you crazy as hell for wanting a man with that much baggage. Hell, he didn't even know his ex-wife used to be a man. At least that's what he says," she replied, twisting her lips in disbelief. "You sure he ain't gay?"

"He's not gay, dang Keke, can you give him a break? According to him she looked like one of the most feminine women he'd ever seen. He says there was nothing about her that indicated that she was a man. I can believe it. Do you see how good these transgender men are looking these day? I can see how a man could easily be fooled.

My bae ain't going nowhere. He played a big part in helping with my recovery. I was in a low place in my life and besides you, Adrian was one of the few people who stood by me when everyone else walked out."

"I can understand that but damn Jen. How do you know he wasn't lying about knowing?

Hell, he grew up around him simply because he was friends with his sister. You mean to tell me *nothing* seemed familiar to him?" Keke asked, cocking her head back, looking at her friend sideways. "Nah, I ain't buying it."

Jennifer responded with a heavy sigh.

Keke continued on, "I know you don't want to hear it, but have you not forgotten what she did to her best friend and the surrogate? And that crazy bitch is still alive. You better watch your back."

"Really, Keke? The woman is laid up in a hospital bed in critical condition. I doubt she will be hurting anyone. Besides, they have police standing guard around the clock outside of her room. Even if she were coherent, which the last time I checked she wasn't, there is no way she is getting past them. When she leaves that room it will be when she's on the way to a jail cell."

Keke shook her head. She couldn't believe how naive her friend was.

"Whatever helps you sleep at night."

Never Can say Goodbye

I felt the warmth of a soft caress on my hand. Without opening my eyes, I instinctively knew that touch. I cracked a smile with the half of my mouth that I had left. It was momma! She'd come to see me. Seeing her help to trigger a few painful memories. I don't recall the details but the last time we were together I was on the run and she and daddy were begging me to turn myself in. After I'd gotten away I never heard from anyone in my family. Not that they could have found me. But I thought for certain they had all cut me off for good.

"Peyton, It's momma," she whispered.

If I could produce tears, I would have broken down at that very moment. I opened my eyes to see the most beautiful person in the word smiling down at me.

"Ma….momma…" I could hardly speak. It felt like I had a mouth full of cotton. The breathing tube had been removed a few hours ago, yet it felt like someone had scraped my throat with a razor blade.

"Shhh, don't try to speak. I just wanted you to know that I was here."

I could feel myself choking up. Everything inch of my body was in pain but seeing her face made everything alright in my world. For a second I thought I'd died and went to heaven. I managed to get out a few more words.

"What are you doing here?"

"I came to see my baby. Regardless of what you have done, or what they may do to you, you will always be my child."

"What they may do to me?" I asked in confusion.

I'd been so drugged and out of it I didn't have any idea what she was talking about. All I knew was that I was in pretty bad shape. I tried my best to piece together more memories but it was all just a blur. None of that mattered at this moment. I had the one person in the world that still loved me here with me.

As I looked up at momma's face I could see the pain. She was still as pretty as ever, but she'd aged. Her hair was thinning and gray and she looked frail. Her eyes told the true story. She looked like she'd spent many nights crying, over me…. It killed me to think that I had placed this much worry upon her and my daddy.

"Peyton, you are my son and I love you. And because I love you I'm not going to sugarcoat the truth. You did some bad things son. You've hurt many people. And you have taken lives."

I suddenly felt the familiarity of her soothing words and gentle touch fading to black. Momma had never been one to mince her words and it seemed as though she was here to serve me up a dose of cold hard reality.

"Do you know what I had to go through to see you? Everyone tried discourage me from making this trip. Your father forbade that I come. There are news reporters outside the hospital hounding me like a pack of rabid dogs. And you have 24 hour police security outside those doors," she announced, glancing at the exit.

Suddenly, my memories came rushing back like a flood gate had been opened. I remembered being on the run and hiding out for all those years with AJ. Speaking of AJ, where was he? How come he wasn't here visiting me? Then it hit me. That little muthafucka shot me! I didn't remember anything beyond that point.

"What are they going to do to me momma?" I whispered.

"I don't know son, but you did some very bad things and you have to pay your debt to society. They have charged you with multiple homicides and the DA is pushing for the death sentence."

Damn! They trying to kill my black ass! I thought.

She could barely get that last sentence out before she broke down in tears. She turned her back so that I couldn't see how tore up she was over the whole situation.

"I need you to understand what you have done and how much pain you have caused this family."

"I do," I replied, my half of lip quivering. "I'm sorry."

"Sorry is not enough for all the damage you have caused. I pray the Lord has mercy on your soul."

Slacking On The Job

"Man, to hell with this. We've been standing here for five hours. I need a break," Officer Bennet griped.

"I feel you, I told you to go take a walk twenty minutes ago," Officer Smith replied.

"So you can get in trouble? I don't think so. You know the Captain will have our ass if he finds out we left this whack job unattended."

Whack job? Who the hell are they talking about? I thought. I could hear the voices of two men talking just outside of my room. This must be the police surveillance momma was talking about.

"Who's going to tell? It's late, so there won't be anyone checking up on us."

"Nah man, I'm good. I'm just cranky because I'm tired as hell. I don't know who I pissed off to get put on this assignment but this is some bullshit."

"Tell me about it. I could be home rubbing on my ole lady's ass," Officer Smith responded.

Officer Bennett glanced around to make certain that the coast was clear. Then he leaned in close to Officer Smith and lowered his voice.

"If you ask me this whole case is a damn waste of the tax payer's money. I mean what the hell are they trying to save that freak for? I say let his ass die already. Better yet, do all of us a favor and yank out all of those fucking tubes and speed up the process."

"You're a cold son of a bitch Bennett," Officer Smith replied, shaking his head.

"Don't give me that righteous act. You can't tell me the thought hasn't crossed your mind. Or have you forgotten how many people this he/she has killed?"

"No, I'm very aware of the damage she's caused. Hell, I want justice for the families more than anybody. My thing is, I want to see them throw the book at her. At least a triple life sentence, with no chance of parole. Let her rot behind bars and think about all the pain and suffering she has caused."

My heart sped up as listened to their words. Until now I never really considered anyone else's feelings while I was doing my dirt. I would be lying if I said that I felt any bit of remorse. I did what I had to do, and anyone who doesn't understand that has never been in love.

A Life Without Regrets

My father would kill me if he knew what I was about to do, but I didn't have a choice. It was either this or resort to doing drugs harder than I already was. However, I doubt even that would take away the misery I felt day and night. I was a tortured soul. It felt like I was losing my mind and I didn't know any other way to fight my demons than to face them.

Since finding out I was the son of a serial killer that used to be a man I have been teetering on the edge of sanity myself.

It was bad enough I had been on the run with my mother my entire childhood, but she also fed me the lies about my father and how he never wanted me. My anger for him grew so deep that by the time we were reunited I didn't want to hear anything he had to say. When I finally took heed to his warnings I was able to expose my mother for the psychopath she really was. Despite my hatred towards her I never thought it would come down to me trying to kill her. However, she made it very clear that day in the kitchen that one of us wasn't going to leave that room alive. It was either me or her.

When I pulled the trigger and watched her head splatter I felt satisfaction. I was finally able to release the explosion of pent up rage I had for her. Minutes later I would feel deep remorse. Unlike her I wasn't a killer.

From the moment my father took me in he has tried to make up for lost time. Both of us were broken down mentally, physically, and emotionally from the whole ordeal.

In the beginning I thought he was worse off than me, and for good reason. True enough I missed out on a normal childhood and the love of my father. But he suffered for seventeen years, not knowing where his child was, or if I was safe. Aside from coming to grips with the fact that my mother was a lunatic, she was on the run with his only son. I don't know how he survived. And although we have yet to bond the way most kids do with their parents. I know it will come with time. I give him mad props for never giving up on me. I will always respect him for that. I believe a part of him will always have some sort of tie with my mother. The good news for him is he was able to overcome and move on with life while I suffer silently.

The moments after my mother was shot were filled with shock, anger, confusion, and pain. Ultimately the wound wasn't fatal. Not only did she live; she haunts my dreams every night. Aside from anxiety and depression, I have insomnia and PTSD. Apart from counseling and my prescribed medication, I often self-medication whenever necessary with alcohol, marijuana, and the occasional Percocet. Up until recently I'd been able to keep my intake at a minimum. As of late I'd been popping four to five Percs at a time.

All of the hatred I once felt for Pebbles was replaced by sorrow over the thought of losing the only mother I've ever known. Even knowing that in the end she would have taken my life if it came down to it, still couldn't erase all the memories that I had with her growing up. Be it good or bad, no matter where we ended up, she always looked out for me. My mother was a fugitive that had me stealing clothes and food to survive but I still loved her. In her own strange way, I know she loved me too. Most people would say she didn't know what love is, and that she was just holding on to me because she had no one else. That may all be true but it doesn't change my feelings towards her.

When I found out that she could possible get the death penalty, the fear of losing her was unbearable. For that reason, I must help her escape. If I knew for a fact that she would receive life without parole, I could live with that. What I can't live with is the idea that I could have possibly saved her life and didn't.

The Prodigal Son

It had been a long ass day of the doctors probing and prodding every orifice on my body. Not only had I successfully completed five reconstructive surgeries to my face and head; I'd finally begun to eat on my own. Just one of the many tasks I had to learn to do again. This was a sign that was bitter sweet. On one hand I was thrilled to know that I was healing up properly. On the other, I dreaded giving up my freedom. I knew there was a prison cell waiting with my name on it. And thanks to this new info from momma, I'd be lucky if I didn't get the death sentence. Of course it would all boil down to my guilt or innocence, but it was a hell of a burden to bear. Once I was done with my evening snack of bland chicken broth and sliced peaches I managed to doze off thanks to the cocktail of drugs that had been administered in my IV.

I was just falling into a deep sleep when I was startled by the sound of the door to my room opening. I was completely caught off guard, considering the nurses and doctors had already made their rounds for the night. I opened my eyes to see AJ standing over me! Everything in me wanted to scream out but the words wouldn't escape my lips. My first thought was that he must have come to finish me off. Terror instantly took over my body as I pissed myself. This is what Fallyn must have felt when I crept in her room that night. As it stood, I was completely helpless. My eye darted around for anything that I could use as a weapon. Not that it would have matter, I was too weak to fight off anyone in the condition I was in.

"Momma," he whispered. "It's me AJ."

I didn't say a word. Instead I lay silent, debating on whether I should push the button for the nurse. Where the hell were the police that were supposed to be guarding me? How the hell did he get past them?

"Don't be afraid. I'm not here to hurt you," he announced in an almost regretful tone.

He looked exactly like his daddy standing there. Except without the rage they'd both exhibited that last time we were together. He slowly walked over to my bed and began to cry. From what I could see he didn't have a weapon. Maybe he was going to kill me with his bare hands. By now I was in a complete state of confusion.

"Get away from me," I cried out in a weak voice.

"Momma I'm sorry I did this to you," he cried. "I came here to apologize and tell you that I love you and that I never meant to hurt you."

Either this shit they was doping me up with had me high as hell, or I was dreaming. First a visit from momma, now this?

"I love you too son. How did you get in here?"

I didn't have time for formalities. There had been a major security breech and I needed answers. He could miss with all the fake emotion. I wanted to know what he was really up to.

"I don't want to talk too much in here, and I can only stay for a minute, but I had to see you. I snuck in when the guards stepped away."

"Ain't that a bitch? I guess protect and serve don't mean shit these days," I fussed.

"Please, keep your voice down," he protested. "If they find out that you are getting better they will release you sooner and we can't let that happen."

"And why is that?" I asked suspiciously. "Did your daddy send you here to finish me off?"

"God no, if he knew I was here he would kill me. He doesn't know anything about what I have planned."

I will admit that my baby boy had grown into a handsome man, but that still didn't erase the fact that I didn't trust him for as far as I could see him. The more I looked at him the memories of our last conversation came rushing back. I remembered all the horrible things he'd said to me. And how he looked at me with hate in his eyes right before he pulled the trigger. Before I knew it I was seething beneath the surface, but I had to play it cool for the moment. I didn't know what to make of the whole situation.

"If you didn't come here to kill me why are you here? I know you didn't go through all this trouble just to tell me that you are sorry."

"Actually I did. And to tell you that I'm helping you escape."

"Boy bye! Yeah, you done lost it forreal." It hurt like hell trying to curl up the half of my mouth that did work. I almost choked from laughing so hard.

"I'm serious. I can't let you go to jail because I don't know what they are going to do to you. I'm getting you out of here as soon as you are strong enough."

I looked him in his eyes to try and read his true intentions. I could tell that he wasn't joking. His solemnity changed my demeanor.

"You're serous aren't you?"

"Yes I'm serious. We may not have had much, but you always took care of me the best you knew how. Now it's time for me to do the same for you."

"So I'm just supposed to believe that you had a change of heart all of a sudden? You must think I'm a damn fool."

"I don't expect you to believe me or trust me after what I've done. But it's been eating me up inside. I tried to hate you, but I couldn't, no matter how hard I tried. I know you aren't perfect. And I don't even want to think about the things that you have been accused of. All I know is I don't want them to hurt you.

He gently placed his hand in mine and kissed me on the forehead. For that moment in time he was my baby again. He wasn't even bothered by my appearance. I had begun to get choked up. I loved him so much but I just couldn't find it in myself to trust him. Everything in me wanted believe him but paranoia got the best of me. Hell, for all I know he and Adrian were plotting against me. However, if he was truly serious about getting me out of here I had to take him up on his offer and let the chips fall where they may. I would deal with the circumstances when they arose. At this point I didn't have much of a choice but to listen to what he was proposing, considering I didn't have anyone else in my corner.

"Alright, you got my attention. So what happens next?"

"The first thing we need to do is find someone who can get you out past everyone undetected. Can you think of anyone that could help us? I mean I will chance doing it myself but it would be much easier if we had help. And it's gotta be someone who won't breath a word of this to anyone."

"The only person that comes to mind is an old friend, Dr Johnson."

"He's a dr.? That's great. He will have no problems coming and going without being noticed," AJ replied with excitement.

"Not so fast," I pondered in thought. "I don't know how to contact him these days. And I'm not certain that he would actually help me." I stared off in the distance as I thought about my last encounter with The Doc. "We didn't exactly end our friendship on good terms."

"Who knows, It's worth a shot. Let me worry about trying to find him."

"I doubt he will help, but I can't think of anyone else. If you do find him remind him of how he once loved me and tell him that I really need his help right now."

Despite all that went down my child still loves me. Adrian couldn't destroy the bond between mother and child.

Ain't Too Proud Too Beg

Who the fuck is this? I thought as I looked down at the unknown number. This was the fourth time they'd called me today. If it were one of my outside patients, they would have left a message. I had a weird ass gut feeling that this was someone I didn't want to talk to.

I couldn't have been more correct. Against my better judgment I answered the next time the phone rang.

"Hello."

"Dr. Johnson?"

"Who's asking?"

"Dr. Johnson if this is you we need to talk," the man on the other end of the line replied.

I was immediately vexed.

"I don't need to talk to anyone who hasn't told me their name. State your business."

"So it is you?" the guy asked.

"Yeah man, it's me state your business!"

I don't know who this fool thought I was, but he needed to hurry up and say what was on his mind before I introduced his ass to the dial tone.

"Doctor, you don't know me but my mother told me to contact you. She said that you might be able to help us."

"Aww shit, now look, I done told both of them females I messed with that I ain't got no damn kids. Don't call me with this bullshit. I'm not your daddy."

Just as I thought. It was somebody that was about to start begging. I cut that shit off with the quickness. As soon as I was about to hang up he spoke again.

"Doctor, I'm not calling to tell you that I'm your son. I'm calling for Mittens."

I could feel the blood rushing from my face. I'm certain that at that moment my black ass was as pale as a ghost. How the hell did Pebbles find me? And what the hell did she want? I looked around to see if anyone was listening and made my way to a secluded corner of the golf course. I don't know who knew this was the pet name that I had for her but I was about to deny everything.

"I don't know no damn Mittens," I spat.

"Do you want me to say her name?" The guy asked. "I was avoiding saying her name over the phone. Is it safe to talk on this line?"

"I don't know what the hell you are talking about, but it's safe to say that this conversation is over."

I hung up the phone, gathered my belongings and headed towards my car. My heart was about to beat out of my chest. Every time my life gets somewhat back to normal this bitch shows up. Not today! I wasn't having it. It was time to get a new number asap! No sooner than I made my way to my vehicle and got in the phone rang again.

"I don't know who you are, or how you got my number, but you need to stop harassing me before I call the police," I threatened.

"Please! Don't hang up. My name is AJ. I'm Pebbles' and Adrian's son. I got your number from a business card I found in my dad's stuff. My mother said you helped her with the surrogate that carried me."

This was the most bizarre shit I'd ever heard. It was bad enough I'd had to deal with the Pebbles, the police and the FBI, now her son? What the hell? I knew helping that bitch would come back to haunt me. They trying to set my ass up.

"Pebbles was a patient of mine but imma tell you just like I told the police. I don't know anything so don't ask. I haven't had contact with her in years, so I can't help you."

"That's funny, according to her you helped to fuel her getaway by giving her money. And you supplied the drug that was found in Fallyn's bloodstream when they found her body."

"I ain't helped nobody do shit! You got me mistaken for somebody else."

I was indignant! I don't even know why I was still entertaining this fool other than wanting to find out what else he knew about me.

"So you didn't give my mother $20,000 when she came to you?"

"I loaned a friend that was in need $20,000 but I don't know what it was used for. And I don't know shit about any drugs. What the hell do you want from me?"

"I want you to help me get her out of that hospital room," he replied. "You are a doctor so it will be easy for you to slip her out."

"Ha! You mean you want me to help her escape? Now why would I do some crazy shit that? You sound like damn fool."

If this truly was her son, he was just as nutty as Pebbles. He may as well have been talking to himself. I didn't want any part of this plan. What the hell do I look like helping Pebbles after all she'd cost me?

"Because you loved my mother once. That's got to count for something. Please, just hear me out. The DA is pushing for the death sentence. Once she's released from the hospital she will go straight to jail."

"And no better for her after all the dirt she has done to people," I snapped, cutting him off.

"If I knew for certain that they were just going to lock her up I could deal with that, but I can't let them kill her," he pleaded.

This nigga was whining like he was the one on death row. I knew they had caught up with her crazy ass. It was all over the news when it went down. All of a sudden a thought came to my mind. Wasn't he the one that tried to kill her?

"Hold up, wasn't you the one that shot her and turned her in? Now you want her to live?"

"Yes and I regret my decision every day. I did what I did based off of emotions. She's the only mother I have ever known. I'm just now bonding with my dad. I can't let them take her from me."

I shook my head at the nonsense I was hearing. This couldn't possibly be happening to me. I had heard enough.

"So lemme get this straight. You shot ya momma and they have her in custody. She hasn't even stood trial yet and you trying to save her from what MIGHT happen?"

"Yes sir."

"All y'all muthafuckas crazy. I don't want any parts of this shit. Lose my number."

With that I hung up on him for good this time.

The Struggle Is Real

I slapped a slice of Domino's meat lover's pizza on a plate and popped cap the on a bottle of Bud light lime. This was supposed to be my relaxation time but this fool had messed that all up. I was appalled that he even took the time to find me and ask me some nonsense like that. I mean it was true, I did love Pebbles at one time, but as of now she was dead to me. I didn't give a shit what happened to her. Especially if it meant bringing the heat down on me. She'd already had a hand in me losing Persia. As far as I'm concerned she can fuck off.

I already had lost so much and was struggling to make ends meet since the club went bust I was laying low and wasn't doing half of the illegal shit that I had did in the past.

I still had my practice. And I scored a lick here and there outside of work, but it was far cry from my past hustles. After the scare Calvin and I had, we were walking on the straight and narrow. My flossin' days were pretty much over. I was swimming in a mountain of debt.

As I sat at my desk shuffling through a stack of bills it suddenly hit me. If I helped Pebbles escape, there was sure to be a huge reward maybe this wasn't such a bad idea after all. It might be worth it if I could get a huge chunk of change out of it. Hell, she owed me that much. The fact that I was even entertaining the thought let me know I had sunk to an all new low. It was risky as hell but if I play my cards right I could be sitting on a load of cash. I mulled over it for two days. The lease on my office was past due. And I owed

Uncle Sam a ton in back taxes. this helped me to make up my mind. I'm going to do it, but they are going to have to play by my rules.

Make Me Do For Love

Damn! This bitch is fucked up!

I almost jumped out of my skin when I saw
Pebbles. I don't know what I was expecting,
considering she'd had half of her head blown
off. When they said that they were just
stitching her up enough to eat and breath
properly; they did just that. Her shit looked
like one of my granny's patchwork quilts.
Aside from reconstructing an eye socket,
nostril hole, and somewhat of a lip; the left
side of her face resembled Fire Marshall Bill
meets The Elephant Man. I was shook by her
appearance to say the least but I didn't let it
show. I put my brave face on and walked in.

AJ had already told her that I would be
coming and I didn't know how she would react

to seeing me. Hell, if anything she should be begging my forgiveness after all the bullshit her trifling ass put me through. However, I wasn't going to press the issue. I needed her to think that I still loved her and that I was truly worried about her wellbeing. When in reality I just needed her to trust me so I could pull of my little scheme.

Before any words were spoken she laughed to herself when she looked up at my head. I know I looked like a damn fool but this latest scalp enhancement was my disguise. It was a blonde Donald Trump cut, complete with a comb over.

"Don't laugh, it's all part of the master plan," I announced. I was paranoid as hell. I checked the room for bugs and cameras before saying another word.

Pebbles looked like she was just as shocked to see me as I was to see her. I thought I was done with her for good after the run in, in Florida. Just goes to show, sometimes life has a funny way of playing itself out.

"You are a sight for sore eyes Doc," she whispered.

I wish I could say the same thing. Yo ugly ass is about to make me vomit, I thought. But I sucked that shit up enough to make small talk.

"It's good to see you again to Pebbles."

I could tell that she was ashamed of her appearance by the way she kept trying to turn the good side of her face towards me. Little did she know; it was one step above the mangled side. As far as I was concerned she was just an ugly person though and through.

"I must look really ugly to you," she said, attempting to pull the blanket over her face.

Here's where I put my Mack Daddy skills to the test.

I walked over to her and gently pulled the blanket away. "You are still beautiful to me Mittens."

"You really mean that Doc?" she replied, batting her right eye.

"I mean it baby girl. I know we have had our differences. But when AJ told me you needed my help I jumped into action."

"Thanks for not giving up on me Doc. You know all those things they are saying about me are lies. And about Florida…. I'm sorry for everything."

"That's all water under the bridge," I replied, waiving my hand.

I was actually telling the truth on that part. True enough, I was pissed about losing Persia behind that bullshit but the material items could and would be replaced as soon as I cashed in on her simple ass.

I could tell that even though I accepted her apology she was still leery of me.

"You weren't saying that when I saw you at the convention with that other woman," she replied suspiciously. "You wouldn't give me the time of day. The only reason I acted out the way I did was because I came to you when I was at my lowest and you outright rejected me. That shit hurt like hell Doc."

No this ugly muthafucka didn't have the nerve to ball up her face like she wanted to cry but couldn't.

I sat on the edge of her bed and looked in her eye. For a second I toyed with the thought of caressing her face but fuck that, a brotha gotta draw the line somewhere.

"That young girl had me sprung. Between that and the success I was having at the time, I was full of myself. But when it was all said and done. I couldn't deny my feelings for you. I never could. I will always love you Mittens."

I think she actually bought what I was selling. I could tell by the way she slid those rough ass hands from under the covers like she thought I wanted them. Little did she know; my hand fetish days were long gone.

"I should have known you would always be there for me Doc," she cooed and placed one of those monkey paws on my knee.

I leaped up so fast I damn near threw my back out.

"You ok Doc," she asked in concern.

"Yeah, I'm cool. You know what your hands do to me, but we need to stay focused. I've come up with an escape plan. I don't want to discuss too many details, but trust me when I tell you that I have everything under control."

A sense of relief came over her face but she was still worried, as she should have been. This was some bizarre shit we were about to pull off.

"Well the first thing I'm worried about the two officers outside my door. What do you plan on doing about them?" she asked.

"Didn't I tell you to let me worry about this? I hate even talking about this here but we can't use the phone so I need you to listen carefully," I instructed.

Pebbles' ears perked up. She straightened up in the bed and prepare to take in every word I said.

"Those two officers that are guarding you are slacking like hell on the job."

"Oh really?"

"Yeah, big time. As we speak one has completely walked away and the other one is trying to get with one of the nurses down at the station. They would be fired on the spot if their boss found out. But we are going to use this to our advantage," I replied rubbing my palms together.

Pebbles nodded her head, "I like where this is going."

"I have already scoped out all the exits and cameras that we need to be aware of. We're going to make this happen at night. I'm going to put a sheet over you and pretend that I'm taking you to surgery we have to move fast."

Pebbles rubbed the stubble on her chin as she thought about the possibilities of what could go wrong.

"I don't know about that Doc," she whispered, shaking her head. So we're just supposed to walk out of here in front of everyone?"

"Hell no, I'm taking you out through the morgue."

Her neck jerked back in disgust.

"Aww hell naw! You mean I got a ride pass dead bodies?"

"You want to get out of here don't you? You'll do whatever it takes to make that happen. As it stands there is an exit on the lower level in the morgue where the hearses pick up the bodies. Everything is all taken care of. Trust me on this."

"Alright, if you say so. I'm down."

"That's my girl. Lay back and get some rest. Your man has everything under control."

What's A Girl To Do?

I couldn't believe AJ was able to talk The Doc into helping. The last time we saw each other it didn't end on good terms. Truth be told I thought he would still be pissed about his little trick Persia. Not to mention I never paid him back a dime that I owed him. And to add insult to injury I cleaned out his hotel room before I dipped. His bitch pressed charged against me. Not that it matters. She could stand in line with the rest of the assholes that want a piece of me. He still looked good despite the tragedy he had on his head. I should have known he couldn't deny his feelings for me. I had that effect on men. It had been a while since I had seen the Doc. I hated that he had to see me this way.

This was one hell of a ride I was on. Not only had my son come to visit me; so did the Doc. The last time AJ and I were face to face he tried to kill me. Granted I didn't give him much of a choice, but I'm his mother! That little asshole should have had some compassion for all I went through to raise him. Ungrateful son of a bitch messed up my gorgeous face for life.

He may have come to his senses now but that still didn't erase what he'd done. I still didn't trust his ass. Ain't no telling what his daddy put him up to. I'm not buying that shit about him not telling him for one minute.

See, now me and The Doc have a different kind of history. We go back way before that test tube baby was even conceived. He was so in love with me I could get anything I wanted out of him. Those type of feelings don't just go away overnight. Personally I never felt that same about him. I had to break ole boy's heart a few times. But seeing as he was the only one in my corner at the moment that I could trust, I may as well take advantage of the situation and use it for all it's worth.

Hard Choices

I hated what I was about to do, but there was no turning back now. The wheels were already in motion. I had successfully gotten Dr Johnson to help us, and so far, everything was going as planned.

It hurt me deeply to betray my father after all he'd done to get to me. The past few days I'd even contemplated calling the whole thing off. I wished like hell I could turn my emotions off. If it were anyone else in the world the decision wouldn't be hard. But this was my mother. She may not be my biological mother, but I love her just the same.

Once this is all over, she can find herself secluded spot to live out the rest of her days in peace. And I'll have the satisfaction of knowing both my parents are alive and safe.

The Escape

The Doc showed up like a thief in the night. I was beyond ready to get the hell out of this place, True enough, I was still weak but I could finish recovering in the hotel. My palms were sweating and my stomach trembled with fear. This was my final chance at freedom. If something went wrong both of us would be up shit's creek without a paddle.

After he slipped into my room he unplugged all the monitoring machines and instructed me to lay completely still. He covered me with a sheet, then checked the hallway to make sure the coast was clear. Once we cleared the room the race was on. I thought he was going to flip me off the table he was moving so fast. We bent the corners with lighting speed, bumping into walls.

"Damn! Be careful," I fussed.

"Shut the hell up," he whispered.

Without seeing my surroundings, I immediately knew when we entered the morgue. The eerie silence and clamminess had me feeling some type of way. The smell of death was prominent despite the efforts used to mask the scent. As I waited for him to pull up with the hearse I couldn't help but think, that could be me, laid up in one of those refrigerators. But as fate would have it, I'm still here.

Moments later I heard the screeching of tires. Seconds after that I was being loaded into the back of the hearse. When I felt that we were a safe enough distance away from the hospital, I sat up.

"Yes!" I squealed with joy. "You did that shit Doc!"

I was free! The adrenal rush had me down right ecstatic.

"Don't celebrate just yet," he replied, looking nervously in the rear view mirror. "All hell is going to break loose once they discover that you are gone. Lay back and chill for a minute."

I could tell that The Doc's nerves were on edge so I obliged. I didn't wanna do shit to throw him off of his game. We were on two totally different pages. While he was worrying about us getting caught, I was still trying to wrap my brain around the fact that I had eluded the police once again. It felt good to have a down ass nigga on my team. I felt like we were on some Bonnie and Clyde shit!

Who else would be riding in the back of a hearse while they still have breath in their body? Pebbles, that's who. They tried to take me down but still I rise! With the help of The Doc and my son I'd successfully escaped. I will admit I was still a bit anxious. At any moment I expected to hear a gang of police sirens behind us, but it never happened. Looks like the Doc had his plan figured out to a tee. After driving several miles, we ditched the death mobile and switched to the Doc's car. I was lightheaded and weak when I tried to stand. There was no doubt that I was going to have to build myself back up before I was able to handle my business. Once he helped me in the car I was overcome with emotion.

"Thank you so much Doc!" I threw my arms around his neck and planted a big kiss on his cheek.

"It ain't nothing," he replied nonchalantly.

"What do you mean it's nothing? You've risked everything to save me and I will forever be grateful. You the real MVP!"

I couldn't understand how he could be so calm and laid-back it a time like this. I was on pins and needles, yet he just helped a criminal elude the police and he remained cool and level headed. He was much harder than I've given him credit for in the past. This look was sexy as hell on him.

"I know you appreciate it Mittens. I'm just trying to stay focused. You're right I have risked everything. Therefore, I have no room for mistakes."

He never took his eyes off the road. He stared straight ahead as he spoke, as though he was looking into his future, I'm assuming a future with me.

He was right, one slip up could cause both of us to get hot lead pumped in our asses. Especially me. They would probably take him to jail but I'm certain they would kill me. I think at this point more people wanted me dead than alive. I understood Drake completely.

"I got enemies, got a lot of enemies, got a lot of people trying drain me of this energy.

Trying to take it away from your girl Pebbles,"
I sang.

The Doc glanced over at me, shook his
head and laughed. I have to admit I've never
been attracted to him, but right now he is my
knight in shining armor.

We turned down a deserted road and drove
past several truck stops. The motel we pulled
up in front of was seedy to say the least. It
resembled a whore infested crack den.
Normally I'd be talking shit, but I knew better
after all we went through to get here. I'm sure
he chose this place because it was low-key and
secluded. Since he had already checked in we
went straight to the room. The walls were a
dingy grayish white. The comforter on the bed
was faded. It reeked of cheap hookers and
cigarette smoke, the carpet was so filthy it was

slick. The dirty, yellowing mini blinds opened to the view of the deteriorating fire escape. Even with all of that it was still better than a jail cell. Quiet as it was kept, it wasn't much worse than the trailer that I stayed in so Lord knows I couldn't complain.

"I know the accommodations are bad but this is the best I could do under the circumstances."

"Doc, please, I'm a free woman thanks to you, and for that I'm, thankful. It won't always be like this. For now, I'm just happy to be out of police custody," I reassured him.

"And we need to keep it that way, for both of us. And the only way that's going to happen is by us being extra careful."

"I love how you take control daddy," I purred. "Just tell me what you want me to do boo."

The Doc sighed. "I'm serious Pebbles. I need you to do exactly as I say," he replied in a stern voice."

Damn, he ain't acting like he's glad to have me out.

Usually by now he would have made some kind of move on me. Imma give him the benefit of the doubt. Hell, my ass was used to being on the run. I had to take into account that this was new for him, I could tell he was scared shitless, as he very well should be.

"I know this is serious, I'm listening."

"First thing, under no circumstances do you leave this room. You are not to answer the door for anyone."

"Got it," I nodded my head in agreement but the truth was I was getting the hell out of here as soon the chance presented itself. "So how do I contact you?"

"I was just getting to that."

He handed me a boost mobile phone.

"AJ and I are the only two that have this number. If you need to speak to either one of us use this phone. Keep all calls brief. Under two minutes if possible. We want to take every precaution to avoid the line being traced."

He went over to the mini fridge and opened it. "I already loaded it with water and juice. And stuff to make sandwiches with. There is more if you need it," he announced, pointing to the extra cases of water.

"So I'm just supposed to make sandwiches? I was on a soft diet in the hospital."

I was so used to being in survival mode that I asked about more food. But the reality was that I knew The Doc wasn't going to let me go hungry. Not to mention the fact that I didn't have an appetite with all the medication I was taking. Speaking of which, he had made sure I had an ample supply of antibiotics and painkillers at my disposal.

"I know sweetness, it's only temporary. I'll be back later with more food. I can't chance coming here every day so we may have to get you some canned goods."

"Canned goods! I don't have a microwave. What am I supposed to do, eat the shit cold?"

I didn't mean to come off as ungrateful but if I was going to be stuck in this hell hole the least I could do is eat good when the mood did hit me. Plus, I needed to get my hands on some cash.

"Damn, I forgot about that," he replied, scratching his head.

"It's fine, I can just order take out."

"Absolutely not! Pebbles, have you been listening to anything that I have been saying? You can't talk on the phone, let alone have someone showing up at this room," he ranted.

"Please Doc, let me at let have some type of pleasure. I don't know how this thing is going to end. Can I at least eat good while I'm stuck here? I promise I won't let anyone in. I'll have the food delivered and just stick my hand out the door to grab it. We don't even have to use a credit card. Do you have any cash on you?"

I pouted and begged till he reluctantly agreed.

"I hope you don't get us caught doing this bullshit," he replied and handed me $200.00. "This should last you for the week. If you must order something, PLEASE cover your face and limit it to once a day."

Bingo! I had officially hit my first lick. He didn't want to do it but at the end of the day it wasn't anymore riskier than him showing up every other day with food. Little did he know I couldn't have given single fuck about some damn food once I got that loot in my hand. I had other plans for this money. Since he was in a generous mood I figured I may as well see what else I could get out of him.

"I promise, and Doc…. can I get one more little thing?"

"What else could you possibly need?"

"A computer."

"Hell naw, that's the last thing you need. You have a TV with cable, watch that."

"But it's going to be so boring. You know don't shit be on. At least bring me a tablet so I can surf the net and play games. Imma be stir crazy up in here after a few days."

"You do know that public wifi is open for anyone to watch what you are doing? Why can't you just read a book?"

At this point he was beginning to get annoyed. I had to do whatever I could to get him to bring me some sort of smart device. I was working on borrowed time and I needed access to the internet. If push came to shove, I may have to suck this niggas dick to get what I need. I don't know how I was gon pull that shit off the way my mouth was set up, but I would work something out.

"I know how to use a private window. And I promise I won't do anything to draw attention to myself. I have a few shows that I can only catch on Netflix, well that is if you sign me in to your account. And you know Candy Crush is an excellent time waster.

Come on Doc. If you can just do this one thing for me... You know what they say about getting head with no teeth? That shit is supposed to be incredible. You wanna test it out?" I purred and attempted to slid my hand up his thigh, only to have him jerk away.

"Hell no!" he replied bluntly.

He had actually pissed me off. That is of course till he agreed to my request.

"Fine, I'll bring you a tablet tomorrow, but that's it."

"Thanks so much, you don't know what this means to me," I squealed from excitement.

Once I had gotten what I wanted I got sentimental on his ass.

"You know it's gets lonely out here Doc. I don't know what I would have done if you hadn't come along and helped my son."

"You know I would do anything for you paws. Like I said before, that other female didn't mean shit to me. I mean I cared about her, but not like I do you. Me and you got history girl. I meant every word that I said back in the car that night."

"I was with Adrian back then, but I always knew you were a good man. Even though I'm not guilty of all that crazy shit they are accusing me of, I just don't understand how you could want to be with someone like me. I'm a fugitive. My face is fucked up….."

"Pebbles, stop it." He cut me off mid-sentence. "I want to be with you because I care about you and you bring excitement to my old boring ass life. Yeah, I know this is some crazy shit I'm doing, but sometimes you have to risk everything in life to get what you want," he replied, placing his hands around my waist. "I want my future to be with you. I'm setting everything in place for us to run away and leave all this shit behind us. That is if you will have me."

That's all I needed to hear. The Doc was still sprung. I understood better than anyone about risking everything for love. Who knows? Maybe we were meant to be together after all.

"Yes! I'm all yours!"

Pebbles At Large

"I swear if they don't catch this bitch I am going to lose it," I said to myself as I watched news.

Pebbles had somehow escaped from the hospital and there was a nationwide man hunt for her. It felt like the nightmare was starting all over again. To make matters worse. I don't know how AJ is taking it. Truth be told I was actually worried about him. He has been detached the past few weeks and I'm not sure why. Lord knows I have done everything in my power to reach him, but he has been through so much already. Having Pebbles as a mother I'm surprised he turned out as stable as he did. Regardless of that fact, I still instructed him not to come home from school. Just in case she decided to show up here. The police and I both felt like he would be safer on campus, seeing as he refused to leave town. I don't think she would chance something that stupid, but who knows the frame of mind she was in.

As of this morning I now had two officers planted outside the house watching, as well as at my job. Half the battle was won. Now if I could only convince Jennifer to take a trip somewhere, anywhere, that would be great, but she wasn't budging.

"I just don't understand why you are fighting me on this," I ranted. "Do you realize how dangerous it is for you to be here?"

"Just as dangerous as it is for you?" she replied with a raised eyebrow. "Look Adrian, I understand the seriousness of the situation but I can't just up and leave my job."

"I can understand that but can't you take a leave? Tell them it's an emergency."

"I'm not doing it. I'm staying here with you We have the police watching. We'll be ok."

Jennifer only had a few bad traits, and one of them was being stubborn. I don't know what I was going to have to do to convince her, but I needed her out of the house asap.

The Tip Off

"Where is this fool at?" I said to myself as I dialed Rob's number for the third time.

I didn't want to leave a message in case he was driving but since he insisted on not picking up I didn't have any choice. He is going to shit a brick when he hears this tea. Just as I suspected it went straight to voicemail.

"Aye Rob, man it's me, Calvin. Pick up your phone. I don't know what you doing but peep this, ya' girl done escaped from that hospital! Just giving you the heads up in case her crazy ass come looking for you. Alright, I'll holla. Call me back when you get this message."

Mastering My Plans

I still had a long way to go as far as healing. My gorgeous face would never be the same. AJ was to blame for that. Hopefully I could stay out of jail long enough for The Doc to do a few extra nips and tucks once we got settled. One would think that with all I was going through that I wouldn't give a damn about my appearance. However, that was the furthest thing from the truth. I'd lost everything. My husband, my son, the few belongings I did have, and now my looks. True enough they had started to fade a bit over the years, but that was from hard living and a bitch being on the run. If I could have found the right man and settled down I would have bounced back in a heartbeat.

My life has come full circle. I have found love, lost it, killed for it, been on the run for it, damn near died for it, yet I'm still standing. The entire United States police force, as well as the general public is looking for me and I'm still standing and I needed to do whatever could to make myself feel beautiful.

I managed to talk The Doc into bringing me a wig and some makeup and he promised to try and get me a glass eye. In the mean time I as all over YouTube practicing the thot bang to try and cover the side of my face. While I was on there I ran across the lip plumping challenge. And you know I had to try that shit. My natural lips were full and pouty, but now I was looking like two face. They say the best revenge after a breakup is looking good. So I needed to get myself together for when Adrian and I met up again.

Even though it had only been a few days, and the law was hot on my tail, I couldn't stay cooped up in this room a moment longer. I couldn't sit around waiting for AJ and The Doc to bring me what I needed I had to be proactive in handling my own business. I covered the side of my face with the hair from the wig and put on a hoodie before I left the room. This would be the first of many times I snuck out. I needed to order some things online and cash just wasn't going to cut it. I found my way to a CVS and discreetly bought a visa gift card. Everything went as planned and I made it back to the room unnoticed. Needless to say I was still a master at what I did.

No Stone Unturned

What the hell has he been up too? I said as I made my way to Rob's front door.

I know he'd received my messages and he ain't been *that* busy at work. As a matter of fact, he hasn't even been in the office in the past few days. I rang the doorbell several times before banging on the side door.

"Rob! Open up, it's me Calvin!"

Nothing.

I dialed his number again while I was standing there. I didn't like this feeling that had come over me.

I remembered that Rob was sprung over Pebbles crazy ass at one time. I prayed to God that he didn't have anything to do with her escaping. I hated to think like that but he was being sneaky as hell lately.

I went back to my car and sat for about an hour to see if I could catch him coming home. I stared at his house and thought about all that we had been through over the years. All the crooked shit we had done together; all the jams we had gotten each other of. When you've know someone for as long as me and Rob have known each other you can't hide shit. This is my best friend. And I know when something doesn't feel right. I finally revved up my engine and pulled off.

"I hope you haven't done anything stupid my friend."

I Got Your Back

"Come on in son." I hugged AJ and let him into the room. "Did you make sure no one followed you here?" I asked, peeping out the window.

"Yes, momma, I was extra careful. You look pretty by the way."

"Thank you baby."

Uhmm hmm, don't be trying to butter me up. I still don't trust yo ass.

"To what do I owe this pleasant surprise?" I asked.

"I just wanted to check on you and see how you were doing. The heat is really coming down and I won't be back to visit because it's too risky."

"I can understand that. You have already gone over and above the call of duty, and I truly appreciate that."

"I love you momma, I'm just doing what I'm supposed to do. I don't know how much longer you can stay here. I'm gonna talk to the Doc about finding somewhere else for you to go till he can get you guys out of town."

Nigga, you can miss me with all that lovey dovey bullshit. I ain't making no moves unless the Doc says it's cool.

"Personally I think I should just stay put. I've lucked out so far being here," I replied.

My blood pressure went through the roof every time I thought about how he turned on me. It was taking everything in me not to slam his damn head into the dresser. I wanted to tell his little ass that he wasn't running shit, and that I was only listening to the Doc, but I had to play it cool for now. He would get his soon enough.

"We can't chance it. The longer you stay in one spot the more you risk being discovered."

I wasn't trying to hear that shit he was talking. I decided to change the subject.

"Ok, I hear you but can we talk about something else.? What did you bring me?" I asked, glancing at the backpack he'd brought with him.

"Some snacks, an electric razor and some toiletries."

"Cool" I replied, rubbing a hand across my five o'clock shadow. I hadn't had my hormones since God knows when and I needed to shave bad as hell.

"And this," he announced, pulling out a glock.

"Oh shit! Nigga caught me slipping!" I screamed and dove behind the bed. I knew his ass was up to no good!

"Momma it's ok. I'm not going to hurt you. I brought this for you."

"I know damn well you did. You brought it to finish off the other side of my face. What did I do to make you hate me so much AJ? All I ever did was try to love you the best way I knew how."

I fucked around and let him get the upper hand on me. I had to talk my way out of this shit before he shot me again.

AJ sighed and walked over to the bed. "Ma will you get off of the floor? I brought the gun for you to use as protection."

"Really?" I asked, peeping at him from behind the bed.

"Yeah ma dang, I don't know how this whole thing is going to turn out. And if it comes down to you having to run again I want you to at least be able to protect yourself."

"Lay it on the bed, and don't make any sudden moves," I ordered.

Once I picked the gun up and examined it I toyed with the thought of splattering his brains across the wall, but he was my son. And for now he was still of some value.

"Thank you son."

"No problem, we gotta look out for each other, right?"

"That's right. Despite all we went through, I did manage to raise you right."

"That you did," he smiled and nodded his head in agreement. "That's why I brought you this as well."

He slid his hand in his pocket and pulled out a stack and handed it to me.

"It's $1000,00. I know it's not much but it's all I could come up with. You're going to need some money to hold you over until we can figure out you a source of income."

My eye damn near popped out of my head when I saw that loot. Maybe he was trying to come legit.

"Hell yeah I need it, thanks!"

After I hid the money and the gun I asked AJ about Adrian. Not that I really gave a damn about how he was doing. I just wanted to pick up on any clues that I could get.

"Have a seat," I said ushering him to the small wooden chair at the desk. "How is your daddy doing?"

"He's good. Of course he's freaking out because you have escaped, everybody is.... They have 24-hour surveillance on his crib."

"Really? And you mean to tell me that you haven't said a word to him about what you have done?" I asked suspiciously.

"Are you kidding me? He would die if he knew that I had any part of you escaping. As far as he knows I'm just as upset as everyone else."

Hmmm, he may be telling the truth. This was a good time to question him about how I was captured the first time.

"Something has been weighing heavy on my mind since I was captured. How did your father know where to contact you?"

AJ shrugged his shoulders and sang like a canary.

"He had been working with that detective dude that was Fallyn's friend."

Just hearing the name Fallyn was enough to send me on a killing spree. That bitch started all this shit by trying to blackmail me. Adrian and I would be celebrating 18 years of blissful matrimony if it weren't for that hoe.

She got exactly what she deserved. As far as that detective Dorian was concerned; I know his bitch ass better not have dropped a dime on me.

"So he told your father where we were?"

"Apparently he was the one that called **Hoodz Most Wanted** and turned you in. Once my daddy found out that he knew more than he was telling, he made him help look for us. He figured he owed him that much for knowing your secret and not saying shit. Once he tracked down where I was going to school it was a wrap."

I could feel my blood boiling. That scum bucket had played part in my demise, which made him the first on my list to feel my wrath.

If he thought, I scared his ass before he was in for a huge surprise.

Time To Get Social

I knew that I couldn't outwardly ask AJ where he and his daddy lived so I had to get creative. Thanks to the internet you could find out pretty much anything you needed to know about a person. My first course of action was creating fake social media accounts. I found Adrian, AJ, The Doc and Calvin's bitch ass on FaceBook. Adrian and AJ didn't really have to many posts set as public. I didn't want to send them a request and arouse their suspicion so I snooped through their friend list for clues. I scrolled down Adrian's page past all the memes and motivational quotes for anything that would help me to locate him. Low and behold I ran up on a picture of him and his new broad. She wasn't me, but she looked alright, I guess. He had the shit tagged WCW, woman crush Wednesday, bitch looked more like Thirsty Thot Thursday.

Since he had tagged her name I was able to go to her page. She had her friends set as private but she had a ton of pics of the two of them together. Judging by the amount of likes and comments she must be pretty popular. I know things ended on a sour note between me and Adrian but it still hurts seeing him with another woman.

"I gave up my life trying to do everything to keep my family and I'm still suffering for it," I spat.

I was salty as hell. If this nigga thinks he's about to move on with a new bitch while my ass is sitting on struggle hill, he got me all fucked up. They all at the park hugged up and shit. This is supposed to be my happy ending. That's supposed to be me laid up with my man, not this hoe. I was so pissed that I was sweating bullets.

After making a few posts I friended several of her mutual friends. One of which was a friend name KeKe. What kinda ghetto name is that? She had several pictures of them together posted as well.

"Ugh! These bitches are parched! Doing all this for some damn likes.

By that night I was Jennifer's friend as well. This was the biggest mistake her dumb ass could have made. Not only was I able to see everywhere she checked in; her personal information was now visible. I went straight to her employment.

"Archdale Family Medicine. Got yo ass!"

Gotcha!

"I knew it!"

I whipped around as I was slipping the key in the door of Pebbles' motel room to see Calvin racing up to meet me. What the fuck was he doing here?

"Knew what? You scared the shit out of me," I replied. I was vexed! Calvin had pissed me off to the fullest with all of his snooping around. This son of a bitch had followed me!

"I knew you had something to do with that broad escaping," Calvin responded matter-of-factly.

My eye's glanced around to see who was watching. Lucky for me the coast was clear. I then snatched Calvin by his collar and drug him into the room before closing the door down behind us."

"Man, what the hell?" Calvin snapped.

"What the fuck is wrong with you? Why you so pressed to keep up with me?" I spewed.

This was a dumb ass move on my part. I probably should have played the shit off and went back to my car but he caught me off guard and I was livid. Hell, a nigga was already on edge to start with. Now I had really screwed up by letting him in the room with Pebbles.

"Doc?" Pebbles called out to me from the bathroom.

I gave her a warning glance before she stepped out.

"Take yo hands off of me!" Calvin jerked himself free from my grip. "I followed you because I was hoping to talk some sense into yo crazy ass!"

"Nigga, I don't know what you talking about. I came here to see a friend. And be alone, so you need to mind your own business and bounce." I announced, leading him back towards the door.

"Bullshit! yo ass went ghost. You been sneaking around and shit. I prayed you weren't stupid enough to have anything to do with that he/she escaping, but my gut never leads me wrong. That's her in that bathroom ain't it?" He replied pushing past me and yanking on the bathroom door. Luckily Pebbles had locked it.

"You overstepping your boundaries Calvin. Now Imma ask you nicely, leave!" I didn't want shit to get physical with him but he had gone too far. If push came to shove, I was going to have lay a few hay makers on him.

Calvin stood in front of me and looked in my eyes.

"Rob, how long have we been knowing each other," he asked softening his demeanor.

I sighed. "Damn near our whole lives."

"Exactly, so what makes you think you can lie to me? After all the shit we went through too clear our name from the club. Not to mention the close calls we done had over the years with all the other shit we been into. I Just hate to see you this old going to jail over a female. You do realize if they catch y'all you going down right along with her? Why would you risk that?"

Everything he was saying was nothing but truth. We had known each other for so long that we could easily see through each other's bullshit. He knew full well that Pebbles was in that bathroom, even if I didn't admit to it. I only hope she had sense enough to not speak or come out until I could get rid of him.

"Because I love her," I replied looking down at the floor to avoid eye contact.

This was a complete lie, but one he would easily believe considering I did once care for her. And the fact that this was the reason he was here in the first place. I couldn't very well tell him that the reason I busted her out of police custody was so I could collect the reward money. Not only because Pebbles was listening; I didn't want this fool trying to cash in on my good fortune. At least if he thought I was a fool in love he might have some loyalty and keep his trap shut until I can cash out and bounce.

Calvin sat down in the arm chair and shook his head in disgust.

"What is it with you and that freakazoid? I mean damn man; I know you ain't that lonely."

"See that's where you have it all wrong. I do get lonely. I know this is crazy. And I've tried to get over her but I'm in too deep. My love for her is too strong to walk away. It was meant for us to be together."

I laid it on thick. I needed to sound convincing to him and Pebbles.

"So what you gon do? Just give up everything and be on the run for the rest of your days with a damn psycho killer? Do you realize how absurd that shit sounds?"

A look of shock and awe painted his face. At this point I didn't need him to agree with me. I just needed him to keep his mouth shut.

"I don't expect you or anyone else to understand my decision. That why I was keeping it a secret. Can you at least be happy for me?"

"That bitch done brainwashed you! Do you know how many people are looking for her?"

He jumped up and pushed me towards the door. "Come on, let's get the hell out of here. Let Big Foot fend for herself and ain't nobody gotta know you had shit to do with any of this."

"Who the fuck you calling Big Foot?" Pebbles screamed, charging from the bathroom.

Shit just got real.

Don't Come For Me

I had heard all that I could take. Who did this bitch made fool think he was, trying to talk The Doc out of helping me? And why the fuck was he here? From the sounds of it he followed him here. My question was why did he let his punk ass in? The last thing we need is witnesses throwing a monkey wrench in our plans. He had given me the signal to stay put. But I couldn't stand by and let Calvin's ole hatin' ass mess our love story up. I had already gone down that road with Adrian. That fool betta' check my history and peep what I did to that bitch that tried to get in my way. And he had me all the way fucked up if he thought he was just going to continue to call me out of my name and thought he was going to get away with it. I charged his ass and tried to slap the taste out of his mouth.

"Pebbles!" The Doc yelled and tried to hold me back.

"Naw, Doc, lemme go! He gon learn today! This fool wanna play with fire, Imma show him, his ass gon get burned fucking with me!"

"Can you please lower your voice before you draw attention to us," The Doc pleaded.

I could tell that Calvin wanted to hit me back but he was too taken aback by my appearance.

"Rob, you betta' call off your Hobbit before I beat her ass!" He hissed, holding his face. "You must be desperate as hell, fucking with a damn cyclops!"

"Can y'all PLEASE calm down before all of us go to jail," The Doc pleaded.

"Oh you got jokes huh? I might have one eye but it's focused on yo ass like a laser beam nigga."

"Pebbles sit down!"

I couldn't believe Doc was yelling at me. He had never raised his voice at me. Despite the issues at hand, he was right. We needed to keep a level head if we wanted everything to keep going smooth. Leave it to a hater to mess everything up. I went ahead and obliged, for now at least. I needed The Doc to think that he was in control. In many ways he was but I needed him to handle his friend.

"I can't believe you gon just let him talk to me like that."

"She's right Calvin. You can't be disrespecting my queen."

"Your queen?" Calvin chucked. "Don't you mean your warthog?

"Fuck you nigga!" I jumped up again but The Doc pushed me towards the bathroom.

"Please go back in here till I get rid of him."

"Fine!"

"Man you a damn fool if you stick around here!" Calvin snapped.

"Look man, I need you to do me a favor."

"Anything man, what is it? I take that back, I meant to say anything within reason," Calvin replied.

"I need you to swear to me that you won't breath a word to this to anyone."

"Maaan" Calvin scratched his head, This was a steep request the Doc was making.

"Come on, I need you to promise. This could be my last chance at love. If I'm making a fool of myself let me find out on my own. But promise me you won't say anything."

Calvin sighed. "I promise."

"Finally!" I said to myself. He had calmed him down and got him to keep his mouth shut, for now at least. As far as I was concerned, he still wasn't to be trusted.

Once The Doc got rid of him I rushed out the bathroom and let him have it.

"Doc how you gon let him up in here!"

"I'm sorry baby. I didn't know he was following me?"

"Damn! Why is he so pressed?"

"Because Calvin and I are best friends. He knows something is off with me. Everything is good now. We don't have to worry about him saying anything."

He was trying his damnedest to try and convince me, but I wasn't buying it.

"I don't understand how you could be so careless knowing what's at stake. You do realize that if he followed you here, someone else could do the same thing?"

I was livid. This dummy had made a mistake that could cost us everything.

"You are absolutely right. That was a huge mistake on my part and it won't happen again. I'm speeding up the plan for us to get out of town. In the meantime, I'm going to lay low at the house, so I won't be back for a few days."

Pebbles' Revenge

I had just finished cleaning up my chin with the clippers that AJ had brought me. I'd stayed up half the night surfing the net and stalking out the pages of my next victims. The wrath I was about to unleash on these fools was going to be epic.

I rolled my eye as I listened to them describe me as a monster. My face was plastered on every news station across the nation. Not to mention there was a $300,000 reward for my capture. Which is all the more reason I didn't need Calvin's punk ass sticking his nose where it didn't belong. Now that there was a bounty out for my head. The last thing I needed was unnecessary witnesses. He might decide that he wanna get loose lips now that some money was involved. He gots to go. He's the first one on my list.

"If you would have stayed a man none of this would be happening," Peyton announced.

Oh God! Not this fool. I already had the chips stacked against me. The last thing I needed was him showing up on the scene.

"Shut up Peyton!"

"You ain't realized that you can't shut me up? I'm a part of you. I don't give a damn about all that shit you put on the outside, I still live inside of you. Everything that's happening to you is because of you living a lie," he replied.

"Go to hell! None of his would be happening if my family and friends would have accepted me like Caitlyn's family did him."

"You are a murdered with split personalities. You don't think that's reason enough not to accept yo crazy ass?"

"So is he! Didn't he run somebody off the road?" You need to look at the thorn in your own eye before you try to judge me."

It took me a minute to realize that his eye *was* my eye. I was back to arguing with myself again. I had to get this shit under control quick. There was no way The Doc could see me like this. So far I'd managed to keep Peyton hidden around him and I wanted to keep it that way. He always seems to show up at the most inopportune times. He popped out several times while I was with Adrian and we see how that turned out.

"Listen to me Pebbles, you are fighting a losing battle and it's causing you to lose the little mind you have left. The only way that you are going to be able to stay free is by changing yourself back into a man," Peyton replied.

I didn't bother answering this time, but he might be on to something. When the time came for me to make my move out of town I needed to do it disguised as a man. And if I was going to live out the rest of my days as a free woman I might have a better chance if I did it as a man. I don't know how The Doc is going to feel about all of this, but this was my life and if he wanted to be a part of it he'd better go along with the program.

One Two Pebbles Is Coming For You

The plan was set. I dressed in sweatpants and a hoodie to disguise the side of my head. I then walked over two miles using the back road to get to a Seven Eleven. This is where I would call for an Uber. I needed some wheels and this was the fastest way I knew to get them. The next thing I needed was a quick and easy way to get rid of the driver. The gun AJ had given me would make too much noise. Lucky for me there was a mini hardware section in the store. I was able to pick up some fishing line and a box cutter. The cashier looked at me strange when I approached the register but she didn't say anything.

I waited impatiently outside until my ride arrived. Once I was inside the vehicle. I unwound some of the fishing line as he drove to the fake destination I'd given him. Once a had a sufficient amount wound off, I cut it with the razor. It would have been easier to just slice his throat with the box cutter, but I didn't want to make a mess by bloodying up the car I would been using. I could tell that he was a bit suspicious by the way he kept glancing at me in the rearview mirror. I never spoke a word. Instead I turned my face towards the window so he couldn't get a full view of the distortion.

"Is this it? He asked, pulling into The Home Depot parking lot.

"Yeah, you can park right here."

I had already mapped this location as being closed down over a year ago.

"Why is the lot so empty? I think they are closed." He asked with confusion in his voice.

As he slowly pulled closer to entrance the overgrowth on the sidewalk and boarded up windows made it evident that the building was vacant.

"Hey this place is abandon......"

Before he could speak another word the fishing line was around his neck. His eyes bulged as he tried to gasp for air. He tried to pull my hands away from his neck. Considering I was much weaker than normal he almost succeeded. I had to literally put my foot in the back of his seat to brace myself.

As the line cut into his flesh his face began to turn purplish/blue from the lack of oxygen. The closer he came to death the harder he fought. Too bad for him, his fight was no match for my rage. A few seconds later his body went limp. I looked around to make sure that the coast was clear and quickly got out the backseat. I then yanked his body from the driver's seat onto the ground and peeled out. I had successfully completed my first kill since escaping. Now that I had transportation there was no stopping me.

The next order of business; find Dorian's bitch ass. I know I said Calvin was first on the list but it dawned on me that Dorian had ratted me out once, he may do it again. Even though he did it anonymously the last time. This time he might take the chance for the reward money. Even though I still couldn't see him calling himself because of the evidence he harbored from Fallyn. That still didn't mean he wouldn't put Adrian up to it since they were buddies and shit. I know that he didn't know where I was hiding out, but AJ did. And the fact that Dorian still kept contact with AJ was a little too close to home. Not to mention I still didn't trust AJ. So if he was up to some shady shit with Adrian and Dorian, this would send a clear message. Back the fuck off!

I used the gps to map his house out. Once I was there I parked across the street to case it out. I needed to know if he was at home so I could take him by surprise.

After sitting for about thirty minutes I finally saw the door to his garage open. He was placing bags in his back seat. After a few minutes he went back in the house without closing the door.

"Got em!"

I know I was playing it close, but there was no time to waste. I had to move fast before he came back outside. I hopped out the car and ran across the street. Once I was in the garage I moved against the wall and hid behind a stack of junk. I debated on getting in the back seat of his car but it was going to be harder to take him out from back there. I spotted a hammer hanging on the opposite side of the garage with the rest of his tools. That shit would have been perfect to bash his head in, but I couldn't chance trying to get to it and he caught me. The box cutter would have to do for now.

I looked down at my hands to see that they were shaking. I was antsy as hell. What was taking him so damn long to come back out of the house? I crept over to the door and saw that he'd left it open.

"Like taking candy from a baby," I said to myself.

It was the perfect setup as far as me getting into the house but it wasn't without risks, considering I didn't know what room he was in.

Once I was inside the kitchen I could hear him moving around in another room. I eased behind the door and waited. From where I was standing I could see that he had luggage waiting by the door.

Looks like I was right on time. His punk ass thought he was gon run.

No sooner than he stepped foot in the kitchen I pounced on his ass.

"Surprise muthafucka! I told you I was coming for yo bitch ass!"

I swung the blade wildly trying to catch his jugular, but he was too fast and strong for me. He threw me off of him.

"Oh shit!" he screamed out.

I did manage to slice his ankle before he tried to run.

"Argh!!!" he cried out as his knee buckled from the pain.

I swiped again for his throat but he knocked the blade from my hand and punched me in the gut.

I doubled over in pain.

Before he could get away I snatched a butcher's knife from the block and plunged it deep into his shoulder.

"Ahhhh!!" he screamed and reached in his waistband, pulling out a snub nose .38.

Ohhh shit! It's time for a bitch to retreat! I thought as I dove out the door.

"Die bitch!!" He yelled as he fired off several rounds, narrowly missing me.

I must have been moving off of pure adrenalin. My ass was dodging bullets like I was in The Matrix. He made his way to the garage and got off a few more shots but it was too late. I was already in my ride and had taken off.

"Shit!!" I screamed and slammed my fist into the dashboard.

I should have known his scary ass was gonna be ready for me. That was sloppy as hell. I definitely needed to polish my skills. I had messed up big time by leaving my weapon. Luckily I was wearing gloves, so it's not like they could lift prints from it. I wasn't worried about him going to the police. But I know for certain he is going to tip off Adrian, who would in turn will alert the damn entire armed forces to come after my ass.

"You done screwed up big time," Peyton announced, shaking his head.

"Not now! I gotta think this shit through," I replied.

Nightmare Returns

"Fuuuuuck!" I screamed and closed down the door to the garage. Hopefully the gunshots didn't draw the attention of too many neighbors. Everyone on the block was mostly at school or work.

I limped back in the house and slammed the door and locked it. My ankle and shoulder was gushing blood. I tried to reach around and pull out the knife but it was in too deep. Not to mention the pain was excruciating.

I tried to tell Adrian that crazy bitch was going to escape, but nooooo he didn't want to listen to me. Thank God I was packing heat. I was able to get off a few rounds to stop her from taking me out.

I grabbed an ACE bandage and wrapped up my ankle to slow down the bleeding. My shoulder was a different story. There was no way I was going to be able to avoid going to the hospital.

I've always maintained the fact that I didn't want to go to the police, and nothing has changed on that front. I'm sure Pebbles knew it, that's why she figured I would be an easy target.

I grabbed sheet from the linen closet and wrapped my shoulder the best I could before I dialed Adrian.

"Hello."

"I told you that nutjob was going to escape!" I panted. "She just tried to kill me!"

"Wait, slowdown, who tried to kill you? Pebbles?" Adrian asked.

"Yeah fool! She came to my house and attacked me!"

"Damn man are you ok?"

"Hell naw! I'm sitting here with a blade in my shoulder."

"Man you gotta get out of there and go to the hospital before you bleed to death. I'm calling the police!"

"Noooo! I keep telling you, no police," I protested.

"Why the hell not? She could have killed you! Ain't no telling where she's headed next."

"I've told yo ass over and over I'm not trying to be an accessory to a crime by harboring evidence. They done questioned me back when Fallyn was killed and I was in the clear. I want to keep it that way. I don't want my name involved in shit! Because you know the first thing they are going to want to know is why she came after me if I have no ties to her. You feel me?"

"Yeah I got you," Adrian replied with an attitude. "I won't mention your name, but they need to know that she was spotted. Did you pay attention to what she was wearing?"

"Hell naw! All I saw was her lopsided ass head. She's looking like somebody beat her ass with an ugly stick. After I bust a few caps at her she hopped in a car and took off."

"Did you at least get a make or a model?"

"All I know was it was black."

"Damn man, you ain't no help," Adrian grumbled.

"What the hell do you want from me? That shit happened fast. I'm just trying to warn you to get your family to safety."

He was starting to piss me off. I tried to call his ass to warn him about Pebbles, and here he was giving me the fifth degree. I didn't need this shit.

"Alright man, I appreciate it. Go take care of yourself."

"I'm about to head out now."

"You good? You need me to drive you?"

"Nah, I'm good."

"Ok, keep me posted."

"Bet"

Once I hung up the phone I headed to the car. By now the blood loss had me feeling lightheaded. I probably should have taken him up on his offer. I knew that I shouldn't be driving but I didn't want the ambulance bill, and I didn't want to draw any more attention.

After I arrived at the hospital they immediately took me in and started asking questions. I told them it was a fail robbery attempt and gave them a fake description. Hopefully this would be enough to throw them off for a while. As for now, I'm getting the hell out of dodge, she won't get to my ass a second time.

Better Safe Than Sorry

"Are you serious?" AJ replied.

"As a heart attack. If she went as far as attacking Dorian she could be coming here next. There's no time for you to get out of town. I need you to check yourself into a hotel and stay put until I give you further instructions. You understand?" I asked firmly.

"Got it dad."

"Good, and watch yourself to make sure no one trails you. Let me know if you need anything."

"Will do. I'll touch base after I check in."

"I love you son."

"Love you too dad."

Now that I had made sure AJ was taken care of, my focus switched to Jennifer. I know she fought me in the past over leaving her job and going ghost for a few days, but now it wasn't up for debate. This time I was going to have to put my foot down if she didn't agree.

Much to my surprise, when I asked this time she agreed to stay with her friend Keke until the police had her back in custody. I didn't tell her about Pebbles attacking Dorian, only because he begged me not to.

The fact that I know I was holding on to evidence that could possibly lead the police one step closer to her vexes me to no end. Hell, I needed to be protecting my family, not Dorian's ass. The only reason I agreed was because I felt a bit of loyalty to him for helping me find my son. If it weren't for that he could kiss my ass. As matter of fact he owed me that shit for knowing that Pebbles had killed Tasha and didn't say anything. The more I thought about it, the angrier I got. I know he's getting out of town behind this shit. It's cool, I'll let him get a head start. Then I'm calling the police.

Settling in

"You need anything?" Keke asked Jennifer as she turned the cover down on the guest bed.

"No, I'm perfect," she replied. "You know I really do appreciate how you are always there for me Keke.

"Girl, I wish you would stop thanking me, chill out," she blushed from lightweight embarrassment. "You know I don't do all that mushy shit."

"I know, you hate mush," Jennifer giggled." But you need to start getting used to it. You already know how I am. Anyway, Adrian wasn't going to rest until he got me out of that house."

"And that right there should tell you something. I called it. I knew they couldn't keep her ass in that room. I won't use this as an opportunity to say I told you so."

Jennifer climbed in the bed and propped herself up on the pillows.

"You most certainly did. I thought it was a long shot. I mean she had half of her head blown off for God's sake. Who comes back from something like that?"

"Haven't you watched enough Jason movies to know that you can't kill crazy? I don't understand why they didn't have her ass strapped down," Keke protested.

"I think they were under the assumption that she was in too bad of shape to do harm to anyone. I guess we were all wrong," Jennifer pondered in thought.

"Well, thank goodness she doesn't know shit about me, or where I live. Otherwise you would have been shit outta luck, friend or not."

"Hush girl," Jennifer laughed.

"You think I'm joking? I'm dead serious. I love you, but ya girl can't roll with the looney tunes," she replied. Anyway, you can stay here as long as you need to. I hope Adrian's got something for her ass if she decides to show up there. I don't know why he didn't come with you. I told you to tell him he was more than welcome."

"You know men. He's hell bent on not leaving his house. He has security around the clock."

"The same kind of security that was supposed to be guarding Pebbles," Keke replied sarcastically.

"Let's hope not," Jennifer laughed. "He does have a gun though he rarely keeps bullets in it. I can stand those things. Personally I wish we didn't even have to have it in the house."

"Please, I'm buying one as soon as I get my income tax money. You can never be too safe. A gun can save your life. He better sleep with that shit under his pillow. You never know what she might do. He needs to be locked and loaded."

"I couldn't agree more."

Making A List And Checking It Twice

Next on my trail of terror was Calvin's punk ass. Dorian was practice, now it was time for the main event. I gotta step my game up for sure. I can't continue to leave jobs unfinished and think I'm about to get away. I need the kill to be quick and flawless.

Once I got to his house I noticed that his car wasn't in the driveway. That was a good sign, but I still had to be extra careful, he could still be there. I couldn't afford to make any mistakes. I watched as his car pulled up. He went inside the house and left right back out.

"I wonder what his ass is up to?"

This was good and bad news. The good news was, I could be certain that he wasn't home, because I'd just seen him leave, the bad news was, he could be coming back soon. I had to move fast and beat him inside.

I looked around to make sure the coast was clear and slipped into his back yard.

"Damn!" I whispered when I saw the doggie door next to his back door.

If he had a dog this could pose a problem. Depending on how big it was. And judging by the size of the opening it had to be for a medium sized breed. And God forbid if it started barking. As of right now I didn't have much of a choice This was my only way inside and I had to chance it. I pulled out my straight razor that I'd ordered off of Amazon and opened the blade. If a mutt did run up, he was gon have to tangle with Pebbles. And I was prepared to slice and dice his ass. Now the next thing I was hoping was if I could fit through here without getting stuck. I had lost a ton of weight, so it just might work.

I decided to do a quick test. If it were in fact a dog in there I wanted to size him up. I flapped the door a few times to see if he would come running or at least start barking. Nothing. Cool, maybe he doesn't have a dog after all. Here goes nothing.

I got on my hands and knees and pushed the front half of my body through the door with success. Just my luck, this sexy rump of mine got stuck.

I twisted and turned, using all my strength to pull my hips through the opening.

"Fuck!"

I was sweating and my mind was racing a million miles a second. There was no way I could let him come back and find me here. The next thing I knew I felt something bump my foot!

"What the hell is that?"

I stopped moving for a split second to hear a dog whining behind me. I turned my head to peek out the glass on the door. There was a mutt standing behind me wagging and growling. Apparently he thought I was playing or his ass was just a wimp. He didn't bark once.

"Where the hell did you come from?" I spat.

I wasn't sure if this was his dog, a stray, or if it belonged to one of the neighbors. All I knew is he needed to be gone.

"Get away!" I said as I kicked my foot back.

This caused him to bounce and play, nudging his nose at my butt, whimpering and growling. The next thing I knew I could feel him sniffing my behind.

"Aww hell naw!" I dropped the blade, kicked my feet and grabbed on to the edge of the door frame to try and pull myself in. If my arms weren't already inside, he would have been history.

"You dumb as hell," Peyton announced.

I didn't even bother to respond. Now was not the time.

I felt the dog's paws on my hips as I wiggled to try and get away. This muthafucka was trying to hump me!

"Get off me!" I yelled and kicked wildly, only causing him to dig his claws in my flesh as he held on.

"He probably thinks you look like a dog," Peyton laughed.

"Shut up Peyton!" I screamed and bucked wildly, finally freeing myself.

Once I was inside I sat on the kitchen floor and caught my breath.

"I'm getting to old for this shit."

I looked outside to see the dog standing his dumb ass by the door panting and wagging his tail. He was huge, it looked like he was some sort of mixed Lab breed, without a mean bone in his body. Obviously he didn't live here because he was way too big to fit through the door, nor did he try. He eventually ran off. Lucky for him I had other tasks at hand or I would have gone after his ass.

Everything else went smoothly. When Calvin got back in the house I was waiting in his bedroom behind the door. When he stepped in, I stepped out and sliced his throat with one fast swoop. He didn't stand a chance because he never saw it coming. I got away smooth and easy despite the massive amount of blood that was spilled. Pebbles was back on top of her game bitches! On to the next one!

All In A Day's Work

"I'm tired of sitting here. I need to take a piss and stretch," Officer Davis complained.

"I feel you man, but Bennett and Smith already let that crazy bitch escape. We can't leave ole boy hanging like that when we're are supposed to be guarding him," Officer Torres replied. "Those fools got suspended without pay. And you know I ain't trying to lose my job."

"Guarding him? He's at work. His girlfriend and son aren't here. They have us sitting like stool pigeons watching an empty house. She ain't gon show up here in broad daylight," Davis replied. "And it's not like we are leaving for good, just a little break."

You probably right, I doubt if we see any action," Torres agreed as he looked around at the deserted street. Aside from the birds tweeting you could almost hear a pin drop.

"Damn right, I'm right. Let's go get some doughnuts!"

I'm Here My Love

Adrian's house was going to be the hardest, or so I thought. He had the police surveying his home around the clock. But after watching their ass for a few hours I realized that they were the same as the lazy ass pigs that were supposed to be guarding me. I noticed that after he left for work, they would take a break and come back just before he arrived home in the evening. I cased them from a distance for a few days to make certain that this was really the routine. Plus, I wanted to get an idea on how the neighbors moved as well. Who went to work at a certain time, who was at home, etc. The fact that I was still free let me know just what I suspected, Dorian wouldn't go to the police. And that Calvin had yet to be discovered.

The next day

Today was going to be different. I was making my move. It didn't appear that Adrian had an alarm system so I could fumble with his windows without worrying about it going off. I just needed to make sure he didn't have any pets. Lord knows I didn't need a repeat of the shit that went down at Calvin's house.

Adrian lived in a beautiful neighborhood. His yard was heavily shaded with huge oak trees and tall privacy hedges that served as the perfect cover.

I wrapped a stone up in the extra shirt I'd brought with me. Hopefully this would help muffle the sound of breaking glass. I quickly slammed it into one of the basement windows near the lock. It shattered with ease. I looked around to see if anyone had heard the noise. I then tossed the rock to the side and wrapped my hand in the shirt to avoid it from being cut as I reached inside and turned the lock. I was in!

I had no plans on killing Adrian, right now at least. For now, I just wanted a look into the man's life that I loved, that once loved me. I couldn't stay long though. I needed to be out before the po po's showed back up.

The house was decorated with an old world style feel to it. Leather sofas, wrought iron and deep, rich woods. It wasn't my taste, but whatever. I looked at the photos on the mantel of him and his new skank. That wanch can't hold a candle to me. My baby was still fine though. I made my way to AJ's bedroom to snoop around a bit, but I didn't find anything interesting.

When I got to the master suite I ran my hand across Adrian's pillow.

"My baby head lays here."

I immediately got pissed when I looked over to Jennifer's side of the bed. If I thought she would be returning I would had rubbed my ass all over that bitch's pillow, but it wasn't worth the time or trouble, considering she was next on my list.

I played around a bit more before I left out the same way I came in, through the basement window, leaving it unlocked. Hopefully he wouldn't go down there before I returned tomorrow.

Can't Put My Finger On It

It had been a long tiring day. All I wanted to do was hop in the shower, grab myself a sandwich and veg out in front of the TV.

The house was super quite without AJ or Jennifer here. I missed them already. It was cool though. I was willing to do whatever I needed to do to keep them safe.

"When did she start arranging the stuff like this?" I asked myself as I grabbed myself a beer from the refrigerator.

The drinks were arranged on the shelf from the largest to the smallest. I suddenly had a flashback of Pebbles doing that shit when we were married and got pissed. I quickly pushed everything around so that it was in no distinct order.

"I'm tripping."

Here I was again letting Pebbles creep her way into my thoughts. Not today. I popped the cap on my Modelo, grabbed my sandwich and headed for the family room without giving her a second thought. I looked out the window to see the unmarked police car still posted up at the same spot as it was when I left for work this morning. All was well on the home front.

The Early Bird Gets The Thot

I got up bright and early. I had a huge day planned. Today was the day Jennifer and her little minion met their maker. I had already staked out her friend's crib and found out that she was staying with her.

"Didn't you know you can run but you can't hide from Pebbles?" I said as I parked and headed towards the house.

The sun had barely come up so I was able to move in the darkness, although it was fading fast. By the time the sun fully rose. I hoped to be inside. Unlike Adrian's place, I hadn't found a way in so this might be a bit of a challenge. That was the very reason I was up at the crack of dawn. Hopefully I could catch these hoes sleeping.

Once I got to the house I crept around outside to see if I could find a way in. Just my luck there was an open window, but it was on the second floor. Now back in the day a bitch would've scaled this house like Spiderman. Now I was too weak and beat down. I had to figure out something else. If push came to shove, I would have to catch one of them on the way out. I made my way to the backyard to see if I could find an unlocked window. Suddenly, the neighbor's dog spotted me and started barking. What is it with these damn dogs?

"Shut yo ass up."

If his little ass blew my cover he was gonna end up as road kill. Just then, a light turned on from the yard where the dog was barking. Someone must have heard him and looked out!

I slipped under the deck and hid there for few minutes to make sure no one saw me. A few moments later the light went back off. Once I felt that it was safe enough, I crept out and peeked in the patio door. Low and behold some dummy had forgotten to lock it. They were making this too easy for me. I slid the door a fourth of an inch and listened. I couldn't hear a thing. Hopefully that meant they were still asleep. I eased it a few more inches until I was able to squeeze in. The house was dark and quiet. My heart raced as I took the first step. The floor was creaky as hell! I needed to find a place to hide. Hopefully this trick didn't have any animals.

I snuck in the den and hid behind the sofa. I still hadn't figured out how I was going to take her friend out. For now, I was just glad to be inside the house, everything else would come naturally. As far as Jennifer's little bitch was concerned; I had other plans for her.

I waited patiently for over an hour. I didn't want to risk going upstairs and they heard me. I wanted to catch one of them coming down. Finally, I heard the floorboards creaking upstairs. One of them was up. Shortly after I heard someone walking, I heard the water turn on in the shower. Now was my chance to make my move.

The noise from the water muffled the sound of me tipping upstairs. I quickly peeked into the bedroom with the open door. This was the master suite, judging by the size and the fact that the bathroom where the shower was running was in here. This must be the friend's room. I couldn't imagine Jennifer sleeping in here if she was just visiting. Perfect!

I eased the bedroom door shut and locked it. I had to make haste. I wanted to catch her while she was still showering. My heart raced as I scanned the room for a weapon. I had my straight razor but It would be hard to hit my mark with her behind a shower curtain.

"Don't fuck up," Peyton whispered.

I totally ignored him and zoomed in on the space heater in the corner. I snatched it up and slipped into the bathroom. This bitch was totally oblivious to my presence, seeing as she was singing. I wanted to kill her ass on that fact alone. It sounded like a damn cat being tortured.

I plugged in the heater and turned it on high before tossing it in the tub and stepping back.

As soon as the electricity hit the water sparks flew. The curtain yanked back as she tried to get out the tub but it was too late. She jerked and thrashed about violently as the current ripped through her body. She tried to turn the water off but her hand was locked on the faucet.

I smiled as I watched her tremble uncontrollably. Foam oozed from the corners of her mouth, her eyes bulging out of her head. There was a loud pop and the lights blew out. She finally expired, hitting her head on the tub when she fell.

Since the power was off and I didn't have to worry about being shocked, I turned off the water.

Just then, I heard the door open at the opposite end of the hall.

"Keke?" a woman's voice called out.

That must be Jennifer!

I unlocked the bedroom door, grabbed the brass candle holder from the dresser and hid.

"Keke, you ok?"

My heart damn near thumped out of my chest as I listened to the footsteps getting closer. Suddenly the bedroom door opened.

"Keke, girl the lights went off. What the hell?" she said as she peeked in the bathroom.

Keke's body lay lifeless in the tub, blood gushing from her head.

"Oh my God!" Jennifer screamed.

When she turned to run from the bathroom she was met with a blow to the side of her head.

About thirty minutes later

"Wake up!" I yelled smacking Jennifer's face.

Her head bobbed back and forth. She wasn't rousing fast enough for me so I doused her face with cold water. "I said wake up!"

When she opened her eyes she looked scared and confused. I had drug her down stairs and tied her to a chair. Her mouth was covered with duct tape in case she tried to scream.

"Oh you finally decided to wake up and join the party?" I asked with a twinkle in my eye.

Tears rolled down her cheeks as she twisted and turned to try and break free, but it was useless. My days serving in the military, I learned how to tie ten different types of knots. Even Houdini couldn't escape my shit.

"Now let's get down to the business at hand, shall we?" I asked pacing the floor in front of her.

"I'm sure you know who I am. In case Adrian hasn't filled you in, you need to Google me bitch. It's little tricks like you that mess up good relationships. I suggest you check my resume and see what happened to the last homewrecker that tried to come between me and Adrian."

She had the nerve to look surprised when I told her that Adrian still loves me.

"Oh you didn't know? He will always love me, and I will always love him. We didn't have no shacking up bullshit like y'all got going on. We had a real bond as husband and wife, something that little thots like you can't take away."

I slapped her upside her head before continuing my rant. I could see the terror in her eyes and that shit gave me a rush.

"I will say one thing, Adrian done damn sure lowered his standards since him and I were together," I sneered, eyeing her up and down.

No this skank didn't try to have a slight smirk on her face.

"Don't get it twisted! Just because my face is fucked up now, I was a bad bitch in my day! Oh and if it makes you feel any better I'm not going to kill you right away like I did your friend. You might be of some value to me so I'll keep you alive for the moment."

It was true, if it came down to it I know Adrian would do anything to get Jennifer back. I could possibly use this against him and hold her ass hostage in exchange for him calling the police off.

Jennifer's expression turned to sadness at the mention of Keke.

"What happened to that smirk? Yeah, that's what I thought."

I left her sitting while I made myself a cup of coffee and rummaged through the room she was sleeping in. I took the money she had in her purse as well as her cell phone. This was about to come in handy. After I took Keke's cash I made my way back down stairs.

I sat in front of her and went through the pictures on her phone. Seeing her and Adrian together set me on edge.

"See this is the shit I'm talking about. I didn't do all the things I did to keep my family together for it to end up like this," I fumed. "I didn't go through all of this so YOU could be laid up in the lap of luxury. That's supposed to be my house!"

I had gotten myself so worked up I was breathing heavy and my eyes were blood shot. Before I knew it I was sweating profusely and hyperventilating. I felt weak and short of breath. I sat on the floor to gather my wits.

"That's what you get," Peyton panted. "Calm yo crazy ass down!"

Jennifer's eyes popped when she heard the change in my voice.

I crawled to the kitchen and found a bag under the sink. I cupped it around my mouth and breathed deeply in and out. I laid on the floor until my heart stopped racing and my breathing regulated. I had given myself an anxiety attack over this shit. Once I got myself back together I went back in the dining room.

"You thought I was down; didn't you bitch? Well I'm back up! Now back to business."

I took Jennifer's phone and scrolled through her text messages till I found Adrian.

"I'm about to have some fun with Mr. Adrian," I announced as I proceeded to write my text.

Good morning boo, I woke up thinking about you.

I pressed send and waited. "Let's see how long it takes him to respond," I giggled.

I could see the displeasure in her face but I didn't give a damn. Adrian I were 'bout to be together again. It was only a matter of time. All I needed to do was set up our little date.

Hey baby, good morning.

"He replied! Aww yea, it's on now! Watch me butter his ass up."

I'm thinking about you. I miss you so much.

I miss you to, but I need you there for just a little while longer. I want you to be safe, he replied.

"Aww, ain't that cute? Adrian says he misses you, but he wants you to stay here so you can be safe. Ha! Too late sucker! Pebbles is in the house! I got yo bitch, now I'm about to come and get me some of that dick!"

I looked over to see Jennifer crying once again.

"What's the matter? You jealous? I know Adrian has that good wood. But you gotta understand it was mine long before it was yours. I'm just here to claim what belongs to me," I snapped.

"Now let's spice things up a bit," I smiled and sent the next message.

I know, it's just that I'm not used to being away from you. I'm so hot, my pussy is soaking wet thinking about you.

Aww shit, I ain't used to you talking like that. He replied.

I rolled my eye. "I should have known he wouldn't be used to your nerdy ass talking freaky. Sit back and watch how a real woman turns her man on."

Before I could respond he sent another message.

What you got on? I got time to get in some phone sex. I'm stroking my dick as we speak.

"No time for phone sex nigga, we keeping this strictly via text."

No time for that. I had something better in mind. Why don't I meet you at the house this evening when you get off? I don't have to stay the night, but I need your body so bad.

I guess that's cool. You got my ass sitting over here on rock hard. How you gon send a nigga to work with blue balls? LOL

"You see that? He's hard and ready for me already. Don't worry baby, I'll be waiting when you walk in the door."

Jennifer kicked her feet and rocked in the chair. She let out a series of muffled noises that I'm assuming were screams. I was just about to slap that hoe to calm her down when another message came through.

"Aww shit! A dick pic!"

I blew that shit up full screen and showed it to her ass.

Your dick looks so good daddy, I want you inside of me right now, I replied.

You keep that up I'm not waiting till this evening. I'm stopping by before I go to work, he replied.

"Oh no, we can't have that." The last thing I needed was him showing up here.

Lol, no time for that. We can get it in good tonight. When you walk in the door I'll be ready. Imma pretend to be sleep and I want you to just take me. I responded.

Aww ok, I see you wanna do a little role playing. I'm down. Hey how you gon leave me hanging?

"Leave him hanging? What's he talking about?" I said to myself.

??? I replied.

Where's my pic at? Don't I get one to hold me over?

"Shit!"

What the hell was I gon do now? I mean I ain't above snapping a picture of myself, but he's been settling for that ole hyena pussy so he might notice. I walked over to Jennifer and showed her the message.

"You see this? This is the result of getting a man hot and bothered. Something you wouldn't know anything about. He wants a pic, so we about to send him one," I announced with a sinister grin plastered my face.

I placed the phone down proceeded to go to work. Jennifer twisted and squirmed as I yanked up her pajama top.

"Hold still bitch!"

Each time I tried to get the picture she leaned her body forward so I couldn't get a good shot. I was done playing nice with her ass. I put the phone down and stepped behind her chair. I placed her neck in the crease where my elbow bent and squeezed. Her face shook and turned beet red as her lungs struggled to find air.

"You ready to act right?" I asked.

She nodded her head.

When I felt she'd had enough I released my grip. "Now let' try this again."

"Damn, I don't know what he sees in these deflated flapjacks, but to each his own. The picture looked a little weird because of the angles and I had to crop out the rope. Hopefully he wouldn't notice.

Here you go boo, I replied.

Nice, but you know what I wanna see, show me that cat.

"Fuck! Well, you know what that means. You gon have to spread em today," I warned Jennifer, "I'm telling you now, I don't want any shit from you."

I undid the rope from her feet so I could slide her shorts down. As soon as her first foot was free the bitch kicked me in the chin. I touched the spot that was wounded and shook my head. "You just don't learn do you?"

I stood up and rag tagged her in the face three times, blacking both her eyes. Blood and snot ran from her nose as she shook with fear. I kicked the chair backwards causing her to hit her head on the wooden floor. By now she was in a daze. I quickly yanked down her shorts and spread her legs.

"When was the last time you shaved? You got a damn wolverine down here. Is that what Adrian is into now?"

I snapped several shots and sent them off.

Where You At?

"Now what the hell has got her so damn busy that she can't answer the phone," I said to myself.

I was mad as hell. I needed this loot and I didn't need her doing anything to jack the plan up. I prayed she was asleep and didn't try anything stupid like leaving out after I clearly warned her not to. It just felt strange as hell that she hadn't picked up in a few hours. One thing that is for certain. Bad news travels fast. So if the police had caught up to her it would be all over the news by now. There wasn't a voice mail set up, not that it mattered. I wouldn't have left a message even if the chance presented itself. As it was, I was trying to lay low. I wasn't going anywhere near that motel room. I had no choice but to wait for her to call me back.

I was beginning to second guess this whole thing, but I'd helped her escape and I was in too deep. I should have followed my first mind and told that son of hers to kiss my ass when he contacted me. Nothing to do now but wait.

Chillax

I called AJ to check in, then popped in the bar for a drink. This wasn't the norm for me these days, especially since I was a recovering alcoholic. However, the past week had been hectic as hell.

I knocked back a few shots of Remy and thought about the night I was about to have with Jennifer. Lord knows I loved that girl. Who would have ever though I would find somebody willing to put up with all the baggage I brought to the table? I know the rumors about me being gay, and possibly knowing Pebbles was a man. I hear people talking around town. Hell, I've even overheard her friend Keke talkin' shit before. That's a hard thing for a straight man to live down.

I gotta hand it to my girl. She has stood by me and never once judged me. After all that we have been though we owed it to ourselves to let our hair down.

Tonight Is The Night

I shut the headlights off and crept down the block, several streets over from Adrian's. After I parked in a secluded area I took off on foot. It was easy for me to make quick work of the basement window, seeing as I had already rigged it from the last time.

I didn't have much time before Adrian arrived so I needed to freshen up and get fine before he got home.

After hopping in the shower I used one of Jennifer's scented body lotions, as well as her perfume. I needed him to think that I was her without a shadow of a doubt. As I began to massage the cream into my thighs, I suddenly felt sad. This was the first time I had really examined them since I'd had been out of the hospital. My long, sexy, lean legs were now skin and bones from so much weight loss, due to not being able to eat. They were covered with huge scars on each from skin grafts taken to replace the skin on the side of my face and head. The wounds I endured represented the life I had led. Much like a solider that had been at war. Before I knew it I started sobbing although no tears fell. I thought about everything I had lost, and what would happen to me if I were captured again.

"Suck that shit up," I said to myself. "You stronger than this girl."

One thing about the queen that I was, I always looked at the bright side. I couldn't let my current situation take away from the fact that destiny had landed me and Adrian back together, and we were about to make love. Just thinking about it brought a smile to my face. I dried my tears and continued getting ready.

My lace fronts are usually on point, but seeing as the side of my head is dented in I need to work some magic, plus I didn't need it flying off in the heat of the moment. I made a swoop to cover my glass eye and used over a dozen bobby pins to secure it to my head. A bitch wasn't about to have her edges looking like Naomi Campbell.

Once I was done with my hair I shuffled around till I found some astro gild in the medicine cabinet and shoved some up inside myself. And worked a few fingers around to loosen things up a bit. My shit hadn't seen a dilator in god knows when. And it was dry as the Sahara Desert. One thing that I was certain of, I was going to be super tight when he got inside me. I know he's going to love that shit. I then slipped into one of Jennifer's red nighties and gave myself the once over in the mirror.

"I'm still stuntin' on you hoes with half of a face!"

I had a few more details to attend to before everything was set. One of which included packing up a few of Adrian's outfits in case I needed them as a disguise. When I finished I slid under the covers and waited for my man to arrive.

You Should Let Me Love You

I sat in the car and took a few pulls off the blunt I'd just rolled. I'd only had a few shots of Remy but it had been so long since I had a real drink, that shit hit me hard. Needless to say, by the time I headed in the house I was completely faded.

Once I was inside I noticed that Jennifer had all the lights out and had lit scented candles. My bae had set the mood and I ready to lay the pipe on her ass for real. She had me horny as hell with all that shit she'd been talking all day. I crept in the bedroom to see that she was playing sleep with her head under the covers. I didn't disturb her. I wanted to follow the plan to a tee. She wanted me to take her by surprise and I was going to do just that.

I stripped down and took a quick shower. After drying off and slapping on some of her favorite cologne I slid under the covers. The way she was bundled up you would think that she didn't want to give me any. I guess playing hard to get was a part of the plan. My shit had gone down a bit from the shower but it didn't take long for it go back rock hard. Jennifer smelled delicious. I slid my hand across her silky ass. For some reason it felt a little different but I couldn't put my finger on it. None of that mattered now. I was about to fuck the shit of her.

"You ready for this dick?" I whispered as I pressed myself up against her warm body. I don't know if she was as aroused I was, but I was wasting no time. I spread her ass cheeks to enter her from behind. Low and behold she was sopping wet.

"Damn you wet as hell," I moaned before attempting to slide inside of her.

It had only been a week since we'd last had sex, but she was tight as hell. I don't know what kind of magic potion she used but I was loving every minute of it. The deeper I got in the tighter she was.

"Your pussy feels so tight and good," I whispered.

It must have felt good to her as well. She let out a deep groan under her breath. Her head was buried in the pillow. Once I was fully inside of her I palmed her ass as she gyrated her hips. That shit was feeling so good, I didn't know how long I was going to last. I wanted to get on top of my baby. I nudged her by her shoulder to flip her over.

Between me being drunk and the shadows caused by the candlelight, I thought my eyes were playing tricks on me. As she slowly turned around it looked like part of her face was missing. Once she lifted up and faced me I got a full view. It was Pebbles!

"You miss this pussy daddy?"

"Ahhhhhh!" I scream out and clocked that bitch in the jaw with an over hand right.

I leaped out of bed so fast that I fell flat on my face. I scrambled to my feet.

"How the hell did you get in here?" I yelled as I reached to turn on the lamp.

"Boy you so silly. Come on back to bed. You know Pebbles always had that snapback," she cooed. "We was already fucking. I don't see what the problem is."

Once the light was on I caught a glimpse of my dick. My shit had shriveled up like a Vienna sausage. My entire crotch was glistening from whatever the hell she'd used to lube up with. I know I should have at least put some drawers on at this point, but there was no time. This muthafucka needed to be dealt with asap! Everything in me wanted dive on this fucker and strangle her with my bare hands. However, I was momentarily in shock from her appearance. She looked like the Crypt Keeper. I hadn't seen Pebbles in years. And the fact was, she looked terrifying. I was snapped back into reality when Pebbles got up on her knees.

"You want me to bend over so you can hit it doggie, like we used to?" she asked, wiggling her hips.

Having sex with your wife and not knowing she is a man was one thing, but after being inside of her again knowing the truth send me into a rage.

I gritted my teeth. "Imma kill yo' ass!"

"Just like you was killing this pussy?" she asked, as she bent over and twerked.

"Ahhhh!!! You muthafucka!!" I lunged at her but I was still a bit intoxicated and missed my mark. She was able to swerve just in time and dodged me.

"Come on Adrian, you know you still want me," she replied, before laughing like a deranged lunatic.

"Bitch ain't nothing cocking up in here tonight but yo head when I blow your shit back!" I yelled and went for the gun I had in my nightstand drawer.

Her voice switched to Peyton. "Is this what you lookin for nigga?" he asked, pointing the barrel at my head. "Put yo fuckin' hands where I can see em!"

I backed off and put my hands in the air. Where the hell were the police that were supposed to be guarding me? My eyes darted over to the dresser where my cell phone was. If I could only get her to let her guard down so I could get to it.

"Don't even think about it. Yo' time is up," Peyton yelled. Then her voice softened as she switched back to Pebbles. "I'm sorry it had to end this way. I still love you Adrian."

My heart fell to my stomach as my life flashed before my eyes.

She pulled the trigger three times. Each time, nothing. The weapon wasn't loaded. It took a few seconds for both of us to actually grasp what had just happened.

"Oh shit," Peyton agonized. He knew he was fucked.

At that moment it was like The Hulk had taken possession of my body. I dove on that bastard and commenced to beating him to a pulp.

"You lowlife piece of shit! You've ruined my life and you have the nerve to step foot in my home?"

Peyton couldn't speak if he wanted to. I was laying haymakers upside his head fast and furious. Before I knew it, I had jumped to my feet and began to stomp the shit out of his ribs. He winced and wheezed for air.

"Adrian please," Pebbles cried out and attempted to block her head from the blows.

I kicked that bitch smooth in her jaw, causing her top denture plate to fly out, cutting her lip. This enraged her.

"You done did it now muthafucka! I paid good money for them teeth!" she screamed," kicking me in my nuts.

"Ugh!!" I doubled over in pain.

Pebbles cracked me over the head with the lamp.

She tried to run but I damn near cut my hand when I snatched her by that steel wool on her head. Lucky for her the shit came off. I flung that shit to the floor and bear hugged her ass, slamming her into the wall. I wanted to look this bitch in the one good eye she did have when I killed her. I wrapped my hands around her throat and squeezed till her eye damn near popped out her head.

"Imma finish what AJ should have done a long time ago."

At this point I didn't even realize my own strength. I spit in her face and proceeded to strangle her so hard, I actually lifted her body off the floor.

As her feet dangled and the blood drained from her face all I could think about was her killing Tasha. I was just about to finish her off when my phone rang. I didn't stop to answer it. But the distraction caused me to slightly loosen my grip. She was able to catch a breath and managed to gasp out a few words.

"You…. might want to… check on Jennifer," she panted.

Just then it hit me. If Jennifer wasn't the one texting me, it must have been Pebbles!

Her eye bucked as I rammed my forearm against her throat.

"Where is she? If you've done anything to her….." Before I could finish she cut me off.

"She's hanging out in the attic."

Hanging in the attic? I thought.

"What the fuck? Did you hang her?"

I was now faced with the dilemma of finishing off Pebbles or finding Jennifer. If she were in fact in the attic she could need my help. And Lords knows every second counts in a life or death situation. On the other hand, if I let this nut go, she was sure to escape once again. The mere fact that I had to make the choice further pissed me off. I punched her ass dead in the nose. She reached up to wipe the blood as it spilled.

"Choose wisely nigga," Peyton announced. "She only has a few more minutes to spare."

"Fuck!" I wailed and took off for the attic, but not before grabbing my phone to call the police while I was on the way.

"Jennifer!" I screamed as I let down the door to the attic.

The stairs creaked loudly as ran up them, leaping three at a time. "Jennifer!"

After I flipped on the light switch I examined every nook and cranny. She was nowhere to be found. Simultaneously I could hear rumbling downstairs. Peyton had pulled one over on me.

"Shit!" I yelled and kicked over a stack of empty milk crates.

I frantically dialed the police and told them what happened before calling Jennifer. I could hear her phone ringing. I ran downstairs and followed the sound to the kitchen. Pebbles had left her phone on the counter. I had a terrible feeling in my gut that something awful had happened to her.

Narrow Escape

That was a close call. That nigga almost broke a bitch down. I can't believe I didn't check that gun for bullets. I had to do some fast thinking. I knew all I had to do was mention Jennifer and his ass would go running after her like the sissy he was. He worked me over pretty bad but I was able to grab the backpack and my denture plate before I got up out of there, but there was no time to get my wig. Adrian pulled out a plug of the little hair I had left when he snatched it off my head.

The sun still hadn't gone completely down. Here my black ass was running down the street in broad daylight, looking like a plucked chicken in a fucking nighty with no drawers. I was running top speed, which didn't seem to be very fast due to my injuries. I had to get back to the car before the heat came down on me.

Just then a little boy around the age of ten zoomed out in front of me on a hover board.

He looked at me strange before yelling out. "Hey! I know you. You're that tran…."

POP!

Before he could finish I clocked him upside his head and snatched his board.

"Won't he do it!" I yelled out.

God continues to bless me despite the haters that stumble on my path. Momma always said when you do right by people, good things always come your way.

It took me a few tries before I got the hang of that shit, but before I knew it a bitch was gliding like Aladdin on his flying carpet! I only had a few more blocks to go before I reached my ride.

Unlike when I was on my way to Adrian's house I drew a ton of attention, considering I couldn't every well hop over fences on the board. Despite it being much faster, I had to take the regular sidewalk. All discretion few out the window when they saw my ass. Quite as it was kept, I was low key pissed that I didn't grab my hair. I couldn't let The Doc see me like this.

Just as luck would have it, I spotted a chick sitting at the bus stop with a twenty inch Remy lace front. I rolled down on her ass and pulled that shit off her head with the quickness and flew by.

"What the hell?" She jumped up and grabbed her head.

Before she had a chance to figure out what happened I was in the wind singing "A Whole New World."

I heard sirens in the distance, but it didn't stop me from safely making it back to my car. This had been one hell of a day.

Not A Moment Too Soon

I called AJ to make sure that he was ok. I told him what Pebbles had done and ordered him to stay put. For some reason he seemed shocked at hearing this news. It was no surprise to me, but I had to realize that AJ was just a child when Pebbles was doing most of her dirt. Up until now all he had only heard about the things she was accused of. Now he was getting a chance to witness them for himself. I'm not sure how he's going to take it.

I broke every speed limit trying to get to Keke's house so I could look for Jennifer. However, when I got there the police had the house surrounded.

"Damn," I said to myself. This didn't look good at all.

I prayed that Pebbles hadn't hurt her. When I saw the yellow tape my heart sank. I tried to bust past the officers that were guarding the door but they insisted on securing the crime scene, therefore I wasn't allowed inside. I told them I was there for Jennifer. I wanted her to know I was there for her. My stomach was in knots when I overhead them say there was one casualty. I breathed a sigh of relief when an officer confirmed that it wasn't Jennifer.

"Where is she?" I asked frantically trying to look over the officer's shoulder into the house. "How come I can't see her?"

"Relax sir, the paramedics are assessing her injuries. And we have a few questions for her."

"Injuries? How bad is she? Fuck questioning! Y'all can do that shit later! Get her to the hospital!"

"Sir, if you don't calm down we are going to have you removed," an officer assured me.

I was a nervous wreck and these fools were telling me to be calm.

I felt horrible when I saw them bring out a body bag with KeKe in it. I shook my head as the tears fell.

"That's fucked up!" I said to myself. All she tried to do was help her friend and look what happened to her. "I can't stand that bitch Pebbles!"

No sooner than I got those words out of my mouth they brought Jennifer out on a stretcher. I rushed over to her.

"I'm here baby, are you ok?"

She nodded her head through a veil of tears. "Keke's dead, she killed her."

"I know, I'm so sorry," I replied, following alongside the stretcher till it reached the ambulance. Other than being knocked in the head pretty hard, it appeared that Jennifer had only suffered minor injuries. They were still taking her to the hospital for observation and further testing.

Once I was certain that Jennifer was ok my focus switched back to Pebbles. That bitch needed to pay for what she had done.

Worst Mistake Ever

I sat outside my dad's house staring at it. I had messed up big time. I thought my mother would appreciate me helping her to escape. With the huge penalty she was facing I thought she would have gone away quietly and not drew any attention to herself. That was the farthest thing from the truth. She had taken lives once again. The bottom line was, there was no stopping the murderer that lived inside of her. I was a fool to think that I could somehow control it by helping her. I popped four Percs and laid my head back on the headrest.

"What the hell have I done?"

Final Destination

My work was finally done. I had taken care of everyone who could put a dent in my escape. True enough Dorian and Adrian were still alive, but at this point I was just happy to get away unscathed. I knew I didn't have to worry about the detective's scary ass trying to go to the police.

Adrian on the other hand posted a bigger threat. I'm certain that he had every police in the state of DC, marked and unmarked on my ass. For that reason, I decided not to go back to the motel right away just in case someone tried to follow me. I found an area secluded by woods and hid out in the car.

Surprisingly, The Doc hadn't tried to contact me. It was for the best. The feds were probably watching him like a hawk right about now. It was a shame that I was going to have to ditch him after all he'd done for me. He was going to be devastated getting his heart broke by me twice, but what was I going to do? I didn't love that man. And at the end of the day he would only slow me down. He says he loves me, but I know deep down he's not about that on the run life. Once I got back to the motel I was gathering my shit and I was bouncing.

After laying low for nearly two days I finally made my way back to the room. Much to my surprise when I opened the door AJ was already inside. It must've been fate.

"AJ? What are you doing here?" I asked.

He stood staring out of the window never turning around.

"I can't believe you did it. I thought if I helped you, you would have gone away quietly and live the rest of your days in peace. But I see now that was a huge mistake on my part I released a monster."

At that moment I realized it was time to kill my son.

"I simply did what I needed to do. I don't expect you or anyone else to understand," I replied as I slowly made my way to the nightstand where I had stashed the gun he'd given me.

The story was going to end differently this time. What I was about to do may sounded cruel but the fact that he was standing here judging me told me all that I needed to know. He couldn't live with his decision to help me escape; therefore, we were back to that day in the kitchen except this time I was the puppet master.

"I'm sorry son," I said as I pointed the gun at him.

"So you're just going to shoot me in my back?" He asked.

For the first time since the operation I was finally able to form a tear.

"I love you son, but I can never trust you. And I can never forgive you for what you did to me. True enough, I forced your hand. But at the end of the day I'm still your mother. And if you could pull the trigger then, you could pull it again if given the chance."

"Even after everything I did to help you?" he asked, choking back the tears.

I shrugged my shoulders, "You should've finished me when you had the chance. I love you AJ."

I pulled the trigger with every intention of blowing his brains out. Instead, all I got were empty clicks. He played me. Just as the bullets were taken out of Adrian's gun he'd done the same thing to me. All I could do was laugh.

"Touché motherfucker," I chuckled.

"Drop it bitch."

I heard the sound of several guns cocking. Without turning around, I dropped the weapon on the floor. This was it, that little bastard had turned me in. The cops had my ass again. Imagine my shock when I spun around to see

Adrian, Dorian, and the Doc all with guns trained at my head. Apparently the gun I'd found at Adrian's house wasn't his only one. I laughed again.

"Just as I suspected I knew I couldn't trust your ungrateful ass," I spewed, cutting my eye into AJ.

"Shut the fuck up!" Adrian barked, busting me in the side of my head with his gun, causing my glass eye to pop out and roll under the bed.

"Oh Lawd! My eye!" I screamed out. Shit was starting to look really bleak as hell from my end.

I began to cry and beg for my life. I could understand Adrian and Dorian coming after me, but The Doc threw me for a loop. I thought he loved me. Just goes to show, men will say anything when they trying to get some ass.

"Doc, please, don't let them do this to me. I thought I was your bae," I pleaded.

"Bae my ass!" he spat. You've caused me to lose the woman I loved, and killed my best friend. Calvin and I have been friends for over thirty years and you snuffed his life in matter of minutes," he fumed. "I never wanted your ass. Fuck you and everything you stand for."

I had never seen The Doc this angry, He was literally foaming at the mouth. My eye then went to Adrian. Maybe I could get some sympathy from him.

"Adrian, don't do this. I'm the mother of your child."

"The child you were just about to kill? You ruin every life you touch. I understand now that I will never have peace until you are dead."

"But I love both of you…"

"You don't know what love is," AJ chimed in. "It's disrespectful for you to even let that shit fly from your mangled ass mouth."

AJ's words cut me like a knife. I'd tried to be the best mother to him that I knew how and this was the thanks I got. True enough, I had just attacked Dorian. And I'm sure he hated me as well but he was my last resort. I had to use my feminine wiles to try and win his sympathy. I looked at him and batted my eye.

"What about you Dorian? Don't let them make you do something you will regret. I know you could use that reward money. Just turn me in and make yourself a nice piece of change."

"Bitch, you ain't cute," he replied. "I've lost many nights of sleep, Fallyn, and my wife because of you. You are like a rabid dog that needs to be put down.

The next thing I knew I was being hit from all directions.

"Aaah!!!" I screamed out in agony and tried to cover myself but the blows came too fast. Each time I recovered from one, I was hit by another, until I eventually fell to the floor where I was stomped by all three men repeatedly.

"Die bitch!" Adrian yelled out before kicking me in my face, causing my jaw to loosen from the socket.

I reeled in agony, spitting up blood. With every stomp I could feel my ribs cracking. Dorian placed his foot on my throat and applied full pressure. His nostrils flared as he glared down at me.

"Lemme finish her off," he spat.

"Not yet, not here," Adrian stopped him.

"Ugh!" I writhed in pain from The Doc slamming his foot into my sternum.

"That's for Calvin!" he snarled.

At this point shit wasn't looking too good for ya girl. If this is how it was going to end I was having the last word on these fuckers.

I sputtered and finally caught my breath enough to speak.

"I got something to say to all you muthafuckas," I announced before hacking up more blood.

"You done said enough! Time to shut this bitch up for good," The Doc replied.

He was about to serve me another blow but AJ stopped him. He had stood back and watched everything from the sidelines like the punk bitch he was. Lord knows I don't know where I went wrong with that boy.

"Let her speak," AJ ordered.

The Doc and Dorian both looked at Adrian for approval. He nodded his head.

The first person I focused my eye on was AJ.

"AJ, you listen to me. And listen to me good. You will NEVER have another mother. You only get one in life. You will never find another soul that loved you like I did. You gon miss me when I'm gone."

He turned his back as the tears started to fall.

"Ack! Ack!!" I coughed a few more times before moving on to Adrian.

"Adrian, I don't care how many women have in your lifetime, you will never replace me. You will never find a love like you and I shared. There's only one Pebbles. We have a bond that can never be broken." Just then my voice switched to Peyton "I will always love you Adrian."

His face twisted in rage. Meanwhile The Doc and Dorian looked on in awe. Up until now, they had never seen Peyton.

"And Doc. You ain't nothing but a muthafuckin hater! You always wanted me for yourself. And when you couldn't have me, you turned on me. As good as I was to you. You'll never find another Mittens dammit."

"Who the hell is Mittens?" Dorian asked in confusion.

The Doc simply waived him off as he began to cry as well.

"And finally, Dorian. Nigga you just couldn't mind your damn business. Just know

Imma haunt you for the rest of your damn days."

That was it. If my life ended now at least I got that shit off my chest.

"Time's up," Adrian said as he motioned the other men.

I was then, gagged, tied by the wrists and blind folded. The next thing I knew I was ordered to get up and walk. I was led from the room to the woods behind the motel.

The night sky lit up from the hail of gunfire that was unleashed. Just like that it was over. My reign of terror had finally come to an end. I lived a crazy ass life, but if given the chance to do it again, I wouldn't change a thing. In the end I know I did it for love.

Epilogue

Little to Pebbles knowledge, once The Doc found out she had killed Calvin, he forgot all about the reward money and vowed revenge for his friend. He called up AJ who was also suffering from his decision of freeing her and they conspired. AJ told Adrian what he had done and where they had Pebbles hidden. He in turn called Dorian who had no problem banding together with them. None of these men were murderers but each of them had a reason for wanting her dead, the main one being, she would never stop killing. For that reason, they decided to take matters into their own hands. She had eluded the police for the last time. It was time for Pebbles to take her final rest.

Adrian: Adrian was finally able to put his life back together knowing that Pebbles was gone for good. He'd almost lost everyone he loved for a second time, but he was spared the heartache. True enough, Jennifer left him after the incident with Pebbles, but they would eventually find their way back to each other. His main focus now is building a life with her and his son. Their relationship was now on the rocks due to the fact that Adrian was having a hard time forgiving him for what he had done. Needless to say, AJ was still his son and he worked on trying to understand why he did what he did. They are taking things one day at a time. Since the police's negligence was the main reason Pebbles was able to get away with so much, Adrian was able to sue the city and win $400,000 in a lawsuit.

AJ: AJ suffered the most after Pebbles was gone. Even though she is dead, the guilt of all the lives she destroyed by him setting her free was eating him up. Despite Adrian's encouragement his life continued on a downward spiral. His addiction to Percs landed him in the emergency room. He is currently receiving counseling as well as drug rehabilitation. With the help of his family he is slowly turning his life around, but he doubts he will ever be the same after Pebbles.

The Doc: The guilt from helping Pebbles escape had taken such a toll on him he started drinking heavily. The fact that his greed was the reason his best friend lost his life was more than he could bear. This resulted in him eventually losing his practice. He is currently trying to pay off the IRS by resorting back to his side hustle of butt injections.

Dorian: Dorian finally told his wife the truth behind his nightmares. She agreed to come back to him, but only if he agreed to counseling. He agreed and is finally getting his life back on track. As it stands he has totally given up the private detective business altogether. He now makes his living selling used cars. Pebbles still haunts his dreams every now and then.

Jennifer: Jennifer took her friend's death super hard, causing her to relapse into depression. She decided that the whole ordeal with Pebbles was more than she'd signed up for and she left Adrian. Ultimately, several months later they both realized that they couldn't live without each other and they got back together. They would go on to get married and have twin girls named Tasha and Keke.

The End

Midnite Love

If you have enjoyed this series, please leave a review. Also be sure to check out my other titles under Midnite Love as well as Lady Onyxx. And as always thank you for the continued support.

Made in the USA
Lexington, KY
25 October 2016